TOEIC

練習測驗（8）

LISTENING TEST

In the Listening test, you will be asked to demonstrate how well you understand spoken English. The entire Listening test will last approximately 45 minutes. There are four parts, and directions are given for each part. You must mark your answers on the separate answer sheet. Do not write your answers in your test book.

PART 1

Directions: For each question in this part, you will hear four statements about a picture in your test book. When you hear the statements, you must select the one statement that best describes what you see in the picture. Then find the number of the question on your answer sheet and mark your answer. The statements will not be printed in your test book and will be spoken only one time.

Statement (C), "They're sitting at a table," is the best description of the picture, so you should select answer (C) and mark it on your answer sheet.

1.

2.

GO ON TO THE NEXT PAGE.

3.

4.

5.

6.

GO ON TO THE NEXT PAGE.

PART 2

Directions: You will hear a question or statement and three responses spoken in English. They will not be printed in your test book and will be spoken only one time. Select the best response to the question or statement and mark the letter (A), (B), or (C) on your answer sheet.

7. Mark your answer on your answer sheet.

8. Mark your answer on your answer sheet.

9. Mark your answer on your answer sheet.

10. Mark your answer on your answer sheet.

11. Mark your answer on your answer sheet.

12. Mark your answer on your answer sheet.

13. Mark your answer on your answer sheet.

14. Mark your answer on your answer sheet.

15. Mark your answer on your answer sheet.

16. Mark your answer on your answer sheet.

17. Mark your answer on your answer sheet.

18. Mark your answer on your answer sheet.

19. Mark your answer on your answer sheet.

20. Mark your answer on your answer sheet.

21. Mark your answer on your answer sheet.

22. Mark your answer on your answer sheet.

23. Mark your answer on your answer sheet.

24. Mark your answer on your answer sheet.

25. Mark your answer on your answer sheet.

26. Mark your answer on your answer sheet.

27. Mark your answer on your answer sheet.

28. Mark your answer on your answer sheet.

29. Mark your answer on your answer sheet.

30. Mark your answer on your answer sheet.

31. Mark your answer on your answer sheet.

Directions: You will hear some conversations between two people. You will be asked to answer three questions about what the speakers say in each conversation. Select the best response to each question and mark the letter (A), (B), (C), or (D) on your answer sheet. The conversation will not be printed in your test book and will be spoken only one time.

32. Why is the man calling the woman?
    (A) To discuss a consultation.
    (B) To provide a business address.
    (C) To promote new service.
    (D) To discuss a repair.

33. What does the woman describe?
    (A) Some window designs.
    (B) A room arrangement.
    (C) A paint color.
    (D) A door knob.

34. What does the man say he has to do?
    (A) Order some items.
    (B) Extend a warranty.
    (C) Offer a discount.
    (D) Mail some samples.

35. Who most likely are the speakers?
    (A) Authors.
    (B) Magazine editors.
    (C) Software developers.
    (D) Bookstore owners.

36. What does the man suggest doing?
    (A) Drafting an article for a magazine.
    (B) Rescheduling a product launch.
    (C) Selling products on the Internet.
    (D) Reviewing a publishing contract.

37. What does the woman object to?
    (A) Ordering additional merchandise.
    (B) Opening another store.
    (C) Changing the business model.
    (D) Spending on advertisement.

38. Why is the woman calling?
    (A) To get driving directions.
    (B) To inquire about a job.
    (C) To make an appointment.
    (D) To check on an order.

39. What does the woman say she will do?
    (A) Call her insurance company.
    (B) Consult another doctor.
    (C) Send an application.
    (D) Visit an office.

40. What does the man explain?
    (A) How to receive a discount.
    (B) How to obtain medical records.
    (C) How to repair an item.
    (D) How to check an account status.

41. What is the woman trying to do?
    (A) Book a hotel.
    (B) Apply for a visa.
    (C) Open an account.
    (D) Send a package.

42. What does the man recommend?
    (A) Reading some instructions.
    (B) Requesting a receipt.
    (C) Using a faster service.
    (D) Choosing a different date.

43. What can the woman do at window 10?
    (A) Speak to a supervisor.
    (B) Receive a voucher.
    (C) Have her photograph taken.
    (D) Pay a fee.

GO ON TO THE NEXT PAGE.

44. What problem does the woman inform the man about?
(A) She lost her computer.
(B) Her luggage did not arrive.
(C) Her password is incorrect.
(D) She missed a flight.

45. What does the man suggest?
(A) Consulting a travel agency.
(B) Using a car service to visit a client.
(C) Joining a meeting by video-conference.
(D) Returning to a hotel.

46. What does the woman plan to do next?
(A) Check for some equipment.
(B) Call an airline.
(C) Report a complaint.
(D) Go to a repair shop.

47. What is the woman preparing?
(A) Some order forms.
(B) Some training materials.
(C) A meeting agenda.
(D) An office newsletter.

48. Why did the woman say, "That's news to me"?
(A) She had already booked a conference room.
(B) She thought a delivery had been made.
(C) She was unaware that a meeting had been postponed.
(D) She believed that policy had changed.

49. What does George agree to do after lunch?
(A) Sign an agreement.
(B) Review a document.
(C) Confirm a deadline.
(D) E-mail a colleague.

50. What type of company do the speakers work for?
(A) A travel agency.
(B) A furniture manufacturer.
(C) An interior design firm.
(D) A clothing retailer.

51. According to the man, what is the main responsibility of the position?
(A) Supervising an assembly line.
(B) Developing a sales strategy.
(C) Managing multiple stores.
(D) Creating product designs.

52. What qualification does Paula mention?
(A) She has a large number of clients.
(B) She speaks a foreign language.
(C) She is familiar with the company's products.
(D) She is an expert in retail trends.

53. What industry do the speakers most likely work in?
(A) Advertising.
(B) Energy.
(C) Tourism.
(D) Fashion.

54. What does the woman say about a new product?
(A) It is comfortable.
(B) It is inexpensive.
(C) It is selling well.
(D) It is being redesigned.

55. What does the man suggest?
(A) Arranging a press conference.
(B) Promoting a special feature.
(C) Initiating product testing.
(D) Giving away free samples.

56. What are the speakers mainly discussing?
   (A) The announcement of a new manager.
   (B) The introduction of a special service.
   (C) Plans for increasing business.
   (D) Procedures for a departmental process.

57. What will happen in July?
   (A) Television advertisements will be launched.
   (B) Client testimonials will be posted online.
   (C) A new Internet bank will be established.
   (D) An advertising agency will be hired.

58. What does the man say will appeal to customers?
   (A) Foreign currency exchange.
   (B) Extended business hours.
   (C) Home loans.
   (D) Online banking.

59. Who is Sophia Rizzo?
   (A) A television producer.
   (B) A car company president.
   (C) An aircraft designer.
   (D) An electrical engineer.

60. Why does the man say, "You're kidding!"?
   (A) He strongly disagrees.
   (B) He would like an explanation.
   (C) He feels disappointed.
   (D) He is happily surprised.

61. According to the woman, what will happen in six months?
   (A) A vehicle will be available for purchase.
   (B) A new television series will begin.
   (C) A business update will be published.
   (D) Production costs will increase.

GOLDSTAR INC.

Name	Departure City
Mr. Alan Wurtz	Atlanta
Ms. Hope Dane-Wallace	Atlanta
Ms. Tara Crover	Denver
Mr. Francisco De La Rosa	Chicago

SAROVAR HOTELS & RESORTS

62. What is the purpose of the woman's trip?
   (A) To negotiate a contract.
   (B) To visit family.
   (C) To attend a trade show.
   (D) To interview for a job.

63. Look at the graphic. Who will arrive next?
   (A) Alan Wurtz.
   (B) Hope Dane-Wallace.
   (C) Tara Crover.
   (D) Francisco De La Rosa.

64. What does the man offer to do for the woman?
   (A) Pay a fee.
   (B) Buy some coffee.
   (C) Carry her luggage.
   (D) Give her a massage.

GO ON TO THE NEXT PAGE.

BROOKFIELD COMMUNITY BULLETIN BOARD

WANTED: Used clothing, books, appliances - please call John Moss at St. Mark's Mission (202) 434-9090

Piano Lessons - Group or private - Best rates - Vicki Wang (202) 213-3444

For Sale: Kommander Weather Chief 6-Person Camping Tent. 6' x 15' - $100 - Good condition. Call Fred Gustavson (202) 213-0771

Volunteer Abroad! Many fulfilling opportunities with Frontier Foundation. (202) 434-2332. Call now! Ask for Beth Grant

Beverage	Price
Latte	2.50
Cappuccino	3.00
Café Mocha	3.50
Café Miel	4.00

65. Why is the woman calling?
(A) To inquire about an item.
(B) To cancel a purchase.
(C) To report a lost item.
(D) To get driving directions.

66. Look at the graphic? Who is the woman speaking with?
(A) John Moss.
(B) Vicki Wang.
(C) Fred Gustavson.
(D) Beth Grant.

67. What does the man say he will e-mail?
(A) An itinerary.
(B) A contract.
(C) Some instructions.
(D) Some images.

68. Why does the man want to try a new drink?
(A) It was recommended by a co-worker.
(B) It was featured in a news report.
(C) He's on a diet.
(D) It has health benefits.

69. What will the man receive with his purchase?
(A) A pastry.
(B) A membership card.
(C) A discount on his next purchase.
(D) A gift certificate.

70. Look at the graphic. How much did the man pay for his drink?
(A) 2.50.
(B) 3.00.
(C) 3.50.
(D) 4.00.

Directions: You will hear some talks given by a single speaker. You will be asked to answer three questions about what the speaker says in each talk. Select the best response to each question and mark the letter (A), (B), (C), or (D) on your answer sheet. The talks will not be printed in your test book and will be spoken only one time.

71. Where is the announcement being made?
(A) On an airplane.
(B) On a tour bus.
(C) At a bank.
(D) At a theater.

72. What service is the speaker mainly explaining?
(A) Personal concierge.
(B) Digital entertainment.
(C) Food options.
(D) Discount tickets.

73. What does the speaker say the listeners should do to use a service?
(A) Open an account.
(B) Sign up in advance.
(C) Download a mobile app.
(D) Enter credit card information.

74. Who is the intended audience of the podcast?
(A) Small business owners.
(B) Corporate trainers.
(C) Civil engineers.
(D) Health-care professionals.

75. What will the speaker discuss on today's show?
(A) Leadership skills.
(B) Real Estate.
(C) Accounting software.
(D) Customer relations.

76. What does the speaker suggest the listeners do?
(A) Enter a contest.
(B) Visit a Web site.
(C) Submit their questions.
(D) Attend an event.

77. Where does the talk most likely take place?
(A) At a trade show.
(B) At a dry-cleaning store.
(C) At a factory.
(D) At a repair shop.

78. What are the listeners advised to do every day?
(A) Use industrial earplugs.
(B) Take inventory.
(C) Meet production quotas.
(D) Clean some equipment.

79. What does the speaker say he will do next?
(A) Give a demonstration.
(B) Distribute a questionnaire.
(C) Introduce a visitor.
(D) Take a short break.

80. What is the purpose of the talk?
(A) To welcome a new employee.
(B) To celebrate a corporate merger.
(C) To remind staff of a policy.
(D) To announce an award winner.

81. What does the speaker say has recently increased?
(A) Local taxes.
(B) Sales leads.
(C) Quarterly travel spending.
(D) Insurance deductibles.

82. What will Harrison Camp be doing next week?
(A) Leading a seminar.
(B) Launching a product.
(C) Attending a convention.
(D) Hiring an assistant.

GO ON TO THE NEXT PAGE.

83. Where does the speaker most likely work?
(A) At a culinary academy.
(B) At an electronics manufacturer.
(C) At an advertising firm.
(D) At an appliance store.

84. Why does the speaker say, "We'll only be asking reviewers about the appearance of the food processor at this point"?
(A) To reassure the listener about a mutual concern.
(B) To show disappointment in a decision.
(C) To suggest a change in product design.
(D) To clarify that a deadline has passed.

85. What does the speaker ask the listener to do?
(A) Give a presentation.
(B) Design a prototype.
(C) Create an advertisement.
(D) Provide a date.

86. Where is the announcement being made?
(A) In an airport.
(B) At a job fair.
(C) At a supermarket.
(D) In a restaurant.

87. What does the speaker invite the listeners to do?
(A) Pick up a coupon.
(B) Get in a line.
(C) Purchase a membership.
(D) Try a sample.

88. According to the speaker, why do the bakery items taste better?
(A) They are made with special equipment.
(B) The beans are roasted locally.
(C) They have no chemical additives.
(D) They were imported from another country.

89. According to the speaker, what has happened in recent months?
(A) Competition from other companies has increased.
(B) Employees have reported low job satisfaction.
(C) Manufacturing goals have not been met.
(D) A product release has been delayed.

90. What should listeners send to the speaker?
(A) A list of client contacts.
(B) A feedback form.
(C) A travel itinerary.
(D) Expense reports.

91. What does the speaker imply when she says, "This is important to our company's future"?
(A) She hopes to find an alternative solution.
(B) She wants to recognize the listeners' efforts.
(C) She wants to accommodate a client's request.
(D) She expects employees to attend a seminar.

92. Who most likely is the speaker?
(A) A tour guide.
(B) A sales clerk.
(C) A scientist.
(D) A corporate executive.

93. What does the speaker suggest that the listeners do before leaving?
(A) Apply for a membership.
(B) Fill out a survey.
(C) Watch a short film.
(D) Go to a gift shop.

94. Why does the speaker say, "Our education specialist, Olivia, is at the front desk"?
(A) To request volunteers.
(B) To indicate where to get information.
(C) To deny a visitor's request.
(D) To explain why she must leave.

Item	Original Price	Sale Price
Dining room table	$1,200	$300
Coffee table	$540	$180
Patio table	$1,000	$250
Kitchen table	$1,100	$275

Weather Forecast			
Thursday	Friday	Saturday	Sunday
Cloudy and humid	Light rain with scattered thunderstorms	Extreme heat	Sunny with onshore winds
High: 85 Low: 75	High: 90 Low: 80	High: 112+ Low: 88	High: 92 Low: 81

95. Look at the graphic. What is the sale price of the table being described?
(A) $180.
(B) $250.
(C) $275.
(D) $300.

96. According to the speaker, why do customers like the table?
(A) It is hand-made.
(B) It is available in many colors.
(C) It is easy to assemble.
(D) It is inexpensive.

97. What does the speaker say can be found on a Web site?
(A) Some instructions.
(B) Some recipes.
(C) A warranty.
(D) A coupon.

98. What event is being discussed?
(A) A grand opening.
(B) A charity walk.
(C) A trip to the zoo.
(D) A music festival.

99. Look at the graphic. Which day was the event originally scheduled for?
(A) Thursday.
(B) Friday.
(C) Saturday.
(D) Sunday.

100. What does the speaker ask the listener to do?
(A) Arrange a meeting.
(B) Contact scheduled performers.
(C) Rent industrial fans.
(D) Print new tickets.

This is the end of the Listening test. Turn to Part 5 in your test book.

GO ON TO THE NEXT PAGE.

READING TEST

In the Reading test, you will read a variety of texts and answer several different types of reading comprehension questions. The entire Reading test will last 75 minutes. There are three parts, and directions are given for each part. You are encouraged to answer as many questions as possible within the time allowed.

You must mark your answers on the separate answer sheet. Do not write your answers in your test book.

PART 5

Directions: A word or phrase is missing in each of the sentences below. Four answer choices are given below each sentence. Select the best answer to complete the sentence. Then mark the letter (A), (B), (C), or (D) on your answer sheet.

101. After interviewing Miranda Song personally, the CEO ------- the position of Senior Creative Liaison specifically for her.
(A) finished
(B) displayed
(C) hosted
(D) created

102. Demolition of Tiger Stadium ------- due to safety concerns of neighboring property owners.
(A) will have postponed
(B) is postponing
(C) postpones
(D) has been postponed

103. Attendance at the meeting is mandatory except for those employees with prior -------.
(A) adjustments
(B) commitments
(C) announcements
(D) conversions

104. Homelessness is frequently described as an invisible problem, ------- its prevalence.
(A) while
(B) until
(C) despite
(D) meanwhile

105. In his letter of reference, Mr. Lopez expressed his ------- for Ms. Grant's ability to work well with others.
(A) admirable
(B) admiration
(C) admiring
(D) admire

106. This Friday, all employees may depart two hours before closing ------- their manager requires them to stay.
(A) either
(B) nor
(C) because
(D) unless

107. Located in Redwood Valley, California, Talent Tech Corp. develops ------- and hiring software.
(A) recruit
(B) recruiting
(C) recruitments
(D) recruiters

108. ------- company policy, all reports of this nature require the signature of your immediate supervisor.
(A) Instead of
(B) According to
(C) Except
(D) Though

14

109. Economic data indicates that ------- no longer favor the Philippines as a priority destination.
(A) tourists
(B) tours
(C) tourism
(D) toured

110. The stories in Drew Cameron's latest collection are ------- the most imaginative narratives of his career.
(A) beside
(B) over
(C) among
(D) upon

111. Employees of Dyson Electronics receive substantial discounts when ------- shop at other stores in the Galleria Mall.
(A) theirs
(B) them
(C) their
(D) they

112. For many years, Orthodox International relied on a body within the company to ------- its products kosher.
(A) certify
(B) associate
(C) affect
(D) replace

113. Because electronic devices are easily -------, extra care must taken during their transport.
(A) damage
(B) damaging
(C) damaged
(D) damages

114. The merger will be finalized when ------- parties agree to the terms.
(A) both
(B) each
(C) so
(D) that

115. The real ------- of customer loyalty programs is the chance to turn good customers into great ones.
(A) value
(B) record
(C) amount
(D) tone

116. We are a modern thinking company who ------- to grow, with 19 locations worldwide.
(A) continual
(B) continued
(C) continue
(D) continually

117. As of January the property was still for sale, with ------- ongoing usage as an office complex.
(A) suggesting
(B) suggests
(C) suggest
(D) suggested

118. In 2004, the corporate headquarters were -------- to Ogden, Utah, to be closer to Hardcastle's mining operations.
(A) stored
(B) stayed
(C) based
(D) moved

119. Jefferson Nordic, producer of world-class skiing equipment, welcomes ------- ideas for improving our products.
(A) specific
(B) specify
(C) specifics
(D) specifically

120. Property management fees can be confusing, and it's difficult to determine what's appropriate and what's -------.
(A) as much
(B) as many
(C) too much
(D) too many

GO ON TO THE NEXT PAGE.

121. At CashMaster, we monitor every transaction, 24/7, to help safeguard ------- fraudulent transactions and email phishing.
(A) since
(B) above
(C) against
(D) within

122. The JBN Elite Award recognizes executives who have not only ------- in sales but who are also brand ambassadors.
(A) excel
(C) excelled
(B) excellent
(D) excellence

123. Outpatient evaluations are ------- scheduled for two sessions of three hours each, although the duration of each session varies.
(A) almost
(B) right
(C) previously
(D) typically

124. The film was released ------- to video and was nominated for the Doomed Planet Award for "Worst Home Video Release."
(A) directing
(B) directly
(C) directs
(D) direct

125. It was then that Mr. Spicer announced he would ------- step down as CEO, effective immediately.
(A) conspicuously
(B) marginally
(C) regrettably
(D) intriguingly

126. The band's new album sold 2.5 million copies worldwide, bringing in a huge profit for Galaxy Records given the ------- production.
(A) inexpensive
(B) unhappy
(C) incomplete
(D) undecided

127. For the ------- majority of private equity investments, there is no listed public market; however, a secondary market is available.
(A) absolute
(B) tentative
(C) ethical
(D) vast

128. Several film directors have appeared in ------- films, sometimes with an uncredited cameo, or sometimes in a more major role.
(A) all
(B) others
(C) their own
(D) each one

129. Qualifying businesses are eligible for billions of dollars ------- tax incentives.
(A) for
(B) with
(C) at
(D) in

130. The area has seen a dramatic comeback as reinvestment has ------- once dilapidated homes into modern urban dwellings.
(A) is transforming
(B) transformed
(C) to transform
(D) transformation

PART 6

Directions: Read the texts that follow. A word, phrase, or sentence is missing in parts of the each text. Four answer choices are given below each of the text. Select the best answer to complete the text. Then mark the letter (A), (B), (C), or (D) on your answer sheet.

Questions 131-134 refer to the following letter.

April 8

Leslie Rosenbaum
Ebony Falcon Supply Co.
1478 46th Avenue
San Francisco, CA 94122

Dear Ms. Rosenbaum:

We are writing to dutifully inform you of a temporary ------- in our
131.
order fulfillment service.

On May 1, we will begin shipping orders from a new warehouse
in Berkeley. -------. The move will take up to two weeks, -------
132. **133.**
which time we may be unable to ship international orders.

------- any delays, please place your next order by April 15. If you
134.
have any questions, please don't hesitate to contact me.

Sincerely,
Otis Clemons
Cox-Franklin, Inc.
Director of Operations, Oakland

131. (A) improvement
(B) disruption
(C) explanation
(D) contribution

132. (A) Pirates have been spotted in the region
(B) Track the status of your order on the USPS Web site
(C) This will allow us to keep a wider variety of items in stock
(D) These will be available at a special price for a limited time

133. (A) instead of
(B) due to
(C) during
(D) below

134. (A) Avoids
(B) Avoided
(C) To avoid
(D) Having avoided

GO ON TO THE NEXT PAGE

From:	Bob Eiger, Vice-Chairman
To:	All Staff
Re:	Professional Development Seminar
Date:	Thursday, May 6

Dear Colleagues,

The first session of our professional development seminar will be held on May 27. The ------- lecture will be led by William Tremonte,
135.
manager of the country's largest hedge fund.

Mr. Tremonte ------- what established technology companies can
136.
learn from venture capitalists. Mr. Tremonte's talk is the only one in the series that tackles venture capitalism. -------.
137.

As you know, Mr. Tremonte is a mover and shaker in the financial world, so we hope all staff will be present.

Nevertheless, you must seek ------- your manager before attending.
138.

Thanks,

Bob Eiger

135. (A) revised
(B) opening
(C) final
(D) wholly

136. (A) discussed
(B) will discuss
(C) has discussed
(D) will have discussed

137. (A) As a student, Mr. Tremonte published an article in a prestigious financial magazine
(B) The rest will deal with various other topics, including branding and customer relations
(C) Many large hedge funds are privately owned
(D) Professional development seminars are gaining popularity in the field of technology

138. (A) approving
(B) who approves
(C) the approval of
(D) having approved

BMTA Public Updates Announced

The Baltimore Metropolitan Transit Authority will ------- a series of service
139.
updates to the public at four meetings at the end of March. -------.
140.

The proposed updates include a new Saturday Penn Station-Midtown route, a new east side flex zone, revised route identification and route adjustments that would create more direct service and one-seat rides.

The meetings ------- at the following times:
141.

March 28 – Baltimore Public Library, 1515 SW 10th Street, Barre Circle
    3:00–5:00 p.m.
March 29 – Quincy Courthouse, 820 SE Quincy Lane
    7:00–9:00 a.m.
March 30 – Garfield Community Center, 1600 NE Rickshaw Road
    11:00 a.m.–1:00 p.m.
March 31 – Avondale East, 455 SE Eutaw Park Blvd.
    6:00–8:00 p.m.

All feedback will ------- the Baltimore Metro Board of Directors for action
142.
on April 20.

139. (A) present
(B) presenting
(C) presenter
(D) presentation

140. (A) The Penn Station-Midtown Line was finished six weeks ahead of schedule
(B) The service changes are designed to modernize Baltimore transit
(C) The commission chair will run for mayor next year
(D) The TMTA has decided to hold monthly meetings

141. (A) did occur
(B) will occur
(C) occurring
(D) occurred

142. (A) reminded to
(B) be considered by
(C) have persuaded
(D) take notice at

GO ON TO THE NEXT PAGE.

From:	wesglavin@royalfarms.com
To:	lougrist@jerseyshorealpacas.com
Re:	Alpacas
Date:	June 12

Dear Mr. Grist,

I represent Royal Farms, one of the largest free-range chicken growers in the mid-Atlantic. Our farm is now in the process of -------

143.

to fresh-range turkeys. We are extremely interested in acquiring a few alpacas to help guard and tend the flocks. Having learned about this ------- at the Maryland State Fair, we contacted the Mid-Atlantic

144.

Alpaca Association, which recommended your breeding program to us. On your Web site, it appears you ------- lease alpacas, but do not

145.

sell them. Initially, we would be interested in buying at least one pair of animals. -------. In the meantime, do you offer tours of your alpaca

146.

farm?

I look forward to hearing from you.

Sincerely,
Wes Glavin
Royal Farms

143. (A) expanding
(B) expanded
(C) expands
(D) expand

144. (A) formula
(B) method
(C) ability
(D) variety

145. (A) currently
(B) patiently
(C) quietly
(D) eventually

146. (A) However, we would be interested in more in the future
(B) If you do, please visit our Web site for more information on our offer
(C) Our farm has been family-owned for over 50 years
(D) Unfortunately, they are no longer in demand at this point

Directions: In this part you will read a selection of texts, such as magazine and newspaper articles, e-mails, and instant messages. Each text or set of texts is followed by several questions. Select the best answer for each question and mark the letter (A), (B), (C), or (D) on your answer sheet.

Questions 147-148 refer to the following customer review.

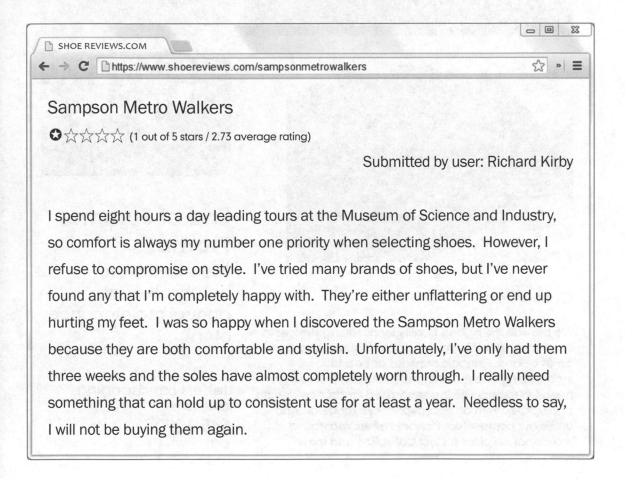

SHOE REVIEWS.COM

https://www.shoereviews.com/sampsonmetrowalkers

Sampson Metro Walkers

★☆☆☆☆ (1 out of 5 stars / 2.73 average rating)

Submitted by user: Richard Kirby

I spend eight hours a day leading tours at the Museum of Science and Industry, so comfort is always my number one priority when selecting shoes. However, I refuse to compromise on style. I've tried many brands of shoes, but I've never found any that I'm completely happy with. They're either unflattering or end up hurting my feet. I was so happy when I discovered the Sampson Metro Walkers because they are both comfortable and stylish. Unfortunately, I've only had them three weeks and the soles have almost completely worn through. I really need something that can hold up to consistent use for at least a year. Needless to say, I will not be buying them again.

147. What is suggested about Mr. Kirby?
(A) His shoe size is not common.
(B) He works in a shoe repair shop.
(C) He recently moved to a new city.
(D) His job requires a lot of walking.

148. What did Mr. Kirby dislike about Sampson Metro Walkers?
(A) Their unattractive style.
(B) Their poor fit on his feet.
(C) Their expensive price.
(D) Their lack of durability.

GO ON TO THE NEXT PAGE.

JEFFERS LANDSCAPING

RATED #1 LANDSCAPER
IN SILVER LAKE

•

FULLY BONDED
BETTER BUSINESS BUREAU™
APPROVED

Our Service

We provide the highest quality landscaping services in Silver Lake. Whether you've got a small back yard or acres of land, Pinnacle provides access to landscaping and maintenance solutions that suit your needs. We specialize in personalized landscape designs and upkeep with an exceptional eye for detail. And unlike our competitors, Pinnacle offers year-round maintenance plans for leaf collection and snow removal.

End of Summer Promo

$50 off with the purchase of an annual maintenance plan

Jeffers Landscaping
Silver Lake
545-1290

---

149. What is indicated about Jeffers Landscaping?
(A) Its employees have experience installing fences.
(B) It is seeking to hire new landscaping professionals.
(C) It operates throughout the year.
(D) It offers lower prices than its competitors.

150. What is NOT offered by Jeffers Landscaping?
(A) Snow removal.
(B) Recycling services.
(C) Landscape design.
(D) Leaf collection.

From:	Fiona Germaine <f.germaine@webfoot.com>
To:	Cole Minn <c.minn@webfoot.com>
Re:	Grady Globetrotter
Date:	April 4

Cole,

I have some great news to share with you! I've been offered a chance work on Grady Globetrotter's new photography Web site, and I'd like you to be involved. Ideally, they would like it to be completed by the end of this month, which doesn't give us a lot of time.

The editor-in-chief, Grady Kuo, has very specific preferences about colors, fonts, layout, and image sizes, which he just sent to me. His e-mail is: g_kuo@gradyimages.com. Drop him a note so we are both up to speed on what he has in mind.

I would also like you to join me on a quick conference call with him tomorrow afternoon at 4:30 so we can go over some of these details. The number is 503-407-2319, and use conference code 78656 to join the call.

Fiona

151. What news does Ms. Germaine share?
(A) She will be attending a trade show.
(B) She will be hiring a photographer.
(C) She has been given a new project.
(D) She has deleted an account.

152. What topic will be discussed during the conference call?
(A) Design elements.
(B) Payment specifications.
(C) Marketing strategies.
(D) Severance packages.

GO ON TO THE NEXT PAGE.

[1:45 PM] Beth Underwood

Buddy, have you completed section seven of the training module yet? I need to format it.

[1:46 PM] Buddy Stoggs

It will be finished as soon as I get the revised safety guidelines from Jennifer Simpson. I'm expecting her to have them ready soon.

[1:47 PM] Beth Underwood

While you're waiting, could you please send me the rest of it? I promised Grant Evans I'd get the final draft to him by the end of the day.

[1:46 PM] Buddy Stoggs

OK. I'll put in a placeholder for the guidelines so we'll all remember where in the training session we're planning to list them.

[1:47 PM] Beth Underwood

That'll work.

153. What has Ms. Simpson been asked to do?
(A) Update some materials.
(B) Schedule a client meeting.
(C) Meet with Mr. Stoggs.
(D) Send a reminder to Ms. Underwood.

154. At 1:50 P.M., what does Ms. Underwood most likely mean when she writes, "That works"?
(A) She will await Ms. Schrote's resignation.
(B) She agrees to Mr. Stoggs's suggestion.
(C) She has approved the training module.
(D) She believes Mr. Evans can complete his work on time.

Questions 155-157 refer to the following form on a Web page.

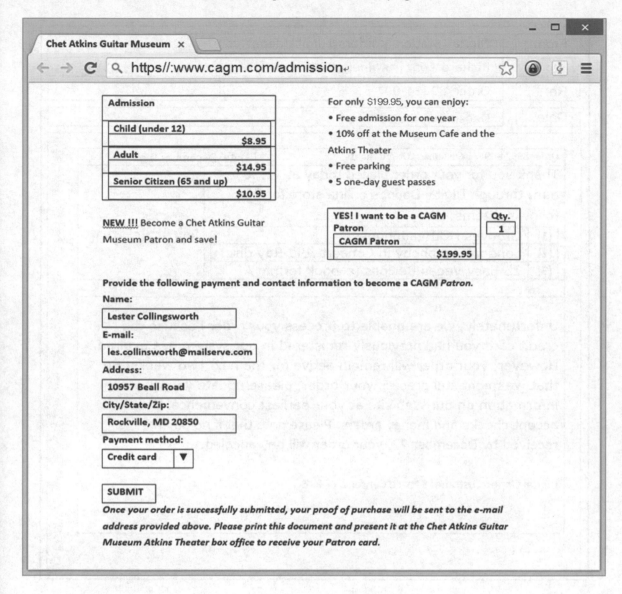

155. How much will Mr. Collingsworth pay?
- (A) $8.95.
- (B) $10.95.
- (C) $14.95.
- (D) $199.95.

156. What is Mr. Collingsworth directed to do?
- (A) Accept an application form.
- (B) Bring his receipt to the box office.
- (C) Enter an access code.
- (D) Reply to an e-mail message.

157. What is NOT mentioned as a benefit available to Mr. Collingsworth?
- (A) Guest passes.
- (B) Free parking.
- (C) Low rates on classes.
- (D) A discount on food.

GO ON TO THE NEXT PAGE.

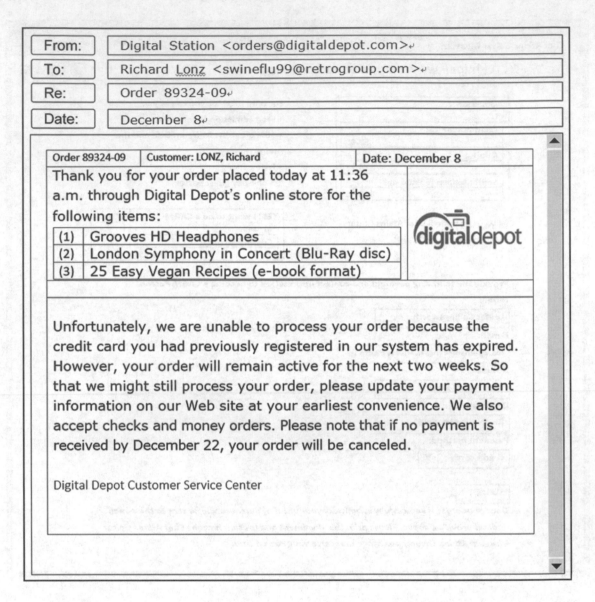

From:	Digital Station <orders@digitaldepot.com>
To:	Richard Lonz <swineflu99@retrogroup.com>
Re:	Order 89324-09
Date:	December 8

| Order 89324-09 | Customer: LONZ, Richard | Date: December 8 |

Thank you for your order placed today at 11:36 a.m. through Digital Depot's online store for the following items:

(1)	Grooves HD Headphones
(2)	London Symphony in Concert (Blu-Ray disc)
(3)	25 Easy Vegan Recipes (e-book format)

Unfortunately, we are unable to process your order because the credit card you had previously registered in our system has expired. However, your order will remain active for the next two weeks. So that we might still process your order, please update your payment information on our Web site at your earliest convenience. We also accept checks and money orders. Please note that if no payment is received by December 22, your order will be canceled.

Digital Depot Customer Service Center

158. Why was the e-mail sent?
(A) To report difficulty in processing a payment.
(B) To explain that items are no longer available.
(C) To inquire about shipping preferences.
(D) To provide an estimated delivery date.

159. What is NOT indicated about Mr. Lonz's order?
(A) It was submitted early in the day.
(B) It must be paid for within two weeks.
(C) It included recorded music.
(D) It will be delivered by December 22.

160. What is Mr. Lonz asked to do?
(A) Update his payment information.
(B) Reply to the e-mail.
(C) Choose different items.
(D) Provide his mailing address.

Questions 161-163 refer to the following e-mail.

From:	Daisy Nimitrov <dnimitrov@genmail.com>
To:	Terry Trevans <strevans@sierrajet.com>
Re:	In-flight meal
Date:	October 23

Dear Ms. Nimitrov,

Thank you for your e-mail. —[1]—.

We at Sierra Jetways are sorry that we were unable to accommodate your special meal request during your flight to Los Angeles International Airport.

To compensate for our error, we would like to offer a *credit of 7,500 miles* to your frequent-flyer account, bringing your total to 34,000 miles. —[2]—.

Please inform us of your preference by replying to this e-mail. You may also contact me at the number below. —[3]—.

Again, we apologize for the inconvenience. We hope that you will continue to choose Sierra Jetways for your future travel needs. —[4]—.

Terry Trevans
Customer Service Manager
Sierra Jetways
800-449-0099 ext. 2874

161. What is the purpose of the e-mail?
   (A) To provide details about an upcoming business trip.
   (B) To advertise a promotion on Sierra Jetways flights.
   (C) To offer compensation to a dissatisfied customer.
   (D) To update information about in-flight meal option.

162. What is suggested about Ms. Nimitrov?
   (A) She requested a specific seat on her flight.
   (B) She bought her most recent ticket at a discount.
   (C) She will inform the airline about her meal preference.
   (D) She often travels with Sierra Jetways.

163. In which of the positions marked [1], [2], [3],and [4] does the following sentence best belong? "You also have the option of accepting a voucher for $150 USD for an upcoming flight with Sierra Jetways or any of our partner airlines."
   (A) [1].
   (B) [2].
   (C) [3].
   (D) [4].

GO ON TO THE NEXT PAGE.

Naperville Business Beat: SCUPPY'S BRINGS BACK PRINT CATALOG

(July 29)—After ceasing print production of its merchandise catalogs several years ago, Scuppy's has decided to bring them back, the store announced this week.

A questionnaire sent to Scuppy's customers last year revealed that the majority favored the return of the paper catalog. Stuart O'Shea, a spokesperson for the store, explained that many customers prefer to browse through an actual hard-copy catalog, even if they later order an item online.

He found that shoppers typically purchase products for the home from the catalog. Unlike their original catalog, which contained over 90 percent of their store merchandise, the new catalog will focus mainly on these items and give limited space to merchandise ordered a little less frequently, such as apparel items.

Media specialist Gordon Heaple noted that print catalogs will serve a purpose in the digital age. "Sometimes it's easier to find the product you want by flipping through real pages," she remarked, "whereas retail Web sites are sometimes difficult to navigate."

According to Mr. O'Shea, Scuppy's new print catalog is scheduled to appear twice this year. It will be mailed to customers and distributed in stores. It will also be available for downloading on Scuppy's Web site.

Scuppy's began as a children's toy store in Darien. Over its 80-year history, it moved to Naperville and expanded into a department store selling a full array of high-quality goods. It boasts a devoted following throughout suburban Chicago, with many customers willing to travel several hours to shop there.

- *by Thad Strock*

164. What is the purpose of the article?
(A) To profile a local company executive.
(B) To report on a business expansion.
(C) To introduce a new Web site.
(D) To announce the return of a publication.

165. The word "noted" in paragraph 4, line 2, is closest in meaning to
(A) went down.
(B) drew.
(C) recorded.
(D) pointed out.

166. According to the article, what did Scuppy's do last year?
(A) It started to offer children's toys.
(B) It developed a new advertising campaign.
(C) It surveyed its customers.
(D) It relocated its headquarters.

167. What is suggested about Scuppy's?
(A) It has acquired many loyal customers.
(B) It is a popular tourist destination.
(C) It sells mainly children's goods.
(D) It has two store locations.

STUDY: LEARNING A FOREIGN LANGUAGE IMPROVES LISTENING SKILLS

By Rondell Forsythe

DETROIT (August 5)—A new study has revealed that learning to speak a foreign language can greatly improve listening skills. – [1] –.

The study, "Hearing Vs. Listening: The Positive Auditory Effects of Foreign Language Acquisition," consisted of observations, interviews, and a series of auditory tests for its 1,000 participants. – [2] –. Fifty participants in the study (adults as well as children) were assigned foreign languages and provided with classes to learn to speak those languages at a basic to an intermediate level over a two-year time frame. – [3] –.

The results of the study showed that those individuals who learned to speak a new language were able to distinguish sounds and pitches more accurately after two years of study. The other participants showed little, if any, improvement. "Learning to speak a foreign language helps a person to develop a strong sense of sound differentiation," explains Jacob Wolfe, one of the study's head researchers. "– [4] –. It is because foreign languages in particular challenge our patterns of expression, I believe we are seeing these enhanced auditory abilities in some participants."

GO ON TO THE NEXT PAGE.

168. What is the topic of the recently published study?
    (A) How age affects the ability to learn a foreign language.
    (B) How learning in a group affects language acquisition.
    (C) How learning a new language affects listening ability.
    (D) How listening to foreign music affects a person's mood.

169. Who is Mr. Wolfe?
    (A) A news reporter.
    (B) A language coach.
    (C) A study participant.
    (D) A leader of a study.

170. In which of the positions marked [1], [2], [3], and [4] does the following sentence best belong?
    "The other 500 did not learn a foreign language."
    (A) [1].
    (B) [2].
    (C) [3].
    (D) [4].

171. What is indicated about the participants in the study?
    (A) All of them were required to learn a foreign language.
    (B) Some of them spoke at an advanced level.
    (C) Only 500 of them had to complete an interview.
    (D) Some of them learned a new language for two years.

Jill Law [9:52 A.M.]

Hi Trent and Byron. I have some unfortunate news about the assistant editorial position. Two of the three finalists for the job backed out before their scheduled second interviews next week.

Byron Ezra [9:55 A.M.]

Why does this keep happening to our department? This also happened the last time, when Trent was hired. Is the benefits package a problem?

Trent Chambers [9:54 A.M.]

Who is left?

Jill Law [9:57 A.M.]

The remaining candidate is Crystal Scott. She's the only one who brought her portfolio to the interview, remember? That work was impressive.
She has all the necessary qualifications, including a master's degree in journalism from Emerson. Should we look for new candidates or go with Ms. Scott?

Trent Chambers [9:59 A.M.]

Byron, the benefits package is comparable to what other companies are offering. The problem is we take too long to decide whom to hire. Candidates are accepting other job offers while we're still making up our minds.

Jill Law [10:01 A.M.]

I couldn't have said it better myself.

Byron Ezra [10:02 A.M.]

Let's offer a contract to Ms. Scott then. She looks good on paper, and she did a great job in her initial interview.

GO ON TO THE NEXT PAGE.

172. What is true about the position?
- (A) It attracted only two applicants.
- (B) It has been advertised for two months.
- (C) It needs to be filled by next week.
- (D) It requires a degree in journalism.

173. At 9:01 A.M., what does Ms. Law most likely mean when she writes, "I couldn't have said it better myself"?
- (A) She wants to interview other candidates.
- (B) She thinks that Ms. Scott will accept the offer.
- (C) She believes that the hiring process is too slow.
- (D) She agrees that the salary needs to be raised.

174. What is suggested about Mr. Chambers?
- (A) He schedules all interviews for the department.
- (B) He has a work schedule different from that of his colleagues.
- (C) He led the job interview with Ms. Scott.
- (D) He is the newest member of the department.

175. What did Ms. Law like about Ms. Scott?
- (A) Her solution to a problem.
- (B) Her previous work.
- (C) Her series of questions.
- (D) Her research on the company.

From:	Grant Thornton, Deputy Director
To:	All Los Angeles Museum of Modern Art staff
Re:	Post-Modern Exhibition
Date:	May 23

✉ Review Quotes (PDF) 18.8k

Dear LAMOMA Staff,

You have my sincere gratitude for your work on the recent "Post-Modern Los Angeles" exhibition. It was warmly received by critics, scholars, and other art professionals. Attached is a selection of review quotes attesting to the show's success. *California Today* called the show "a brilliant gem of L.A.'s Post-Modern movement." Quite surprisingly, it was rated 10 out of 10 by L.A.'s most outspoken critic, Yasuhiro Sakei, an unprecedented achievement.

Because of the exhibition's success, the LAMOMA Board of Trustees has voted to fund an upgrade to our museum's Sculpture Atrium. Thus, we can continue to curate the most exceptional new works of the West Coast art scene. Renovations to the Atrium will commence early next year.

Over the past two weeks, our new chief curator, Amanda Leiber, has been planning the summer exhibition schedule with me. Please join us for an all-staff meeting on April 16 in Conference Room B at 9:45 a.m. Amanda will introduce herself and present our ideas.

Keep up the great work!

Grant Thornton

GO ON TO THE NEXT PAGE.

"Both a breathtaking wonder and a sublime treat."

—Dasmarinas Savoy, Art Critic, *Los Angeles Tribune*

"If you see one show this year, make sure it's this one."

—Anthony Hicks, *Bel-Air Journal of Design*

"A brilliant gem of L.A.'s post-modern movement."

—Delphine Abebe, *California Today*

10/10. In fact, if I could say 11/10, I would."

—Yasuhiro Sakei, *Cutting Edge L.A.*

"The kind of exhibition that inspires and invigorates."

—Joe Pizzini, *Downtown*

---

176. What is the purpose of the e-mail?
(A) To notify personnel about a cancelled exhibition.
(B) To encourage workers to improve their skills.
(C) To advise staff about a job opening.
(D) To praise employees for their work.

177. What does Mr. Thornton ask recipients of the e-mail to do?
(A) Work extra hours.
(B) Complete a questionnaire.
(C) Attend a meeting.
(D) Write a review.

178. What reviewer's rating particularly pleases Mr. Thornton?
(A) Ms. Savoy's.
(B) Mr. Hicks's.
(C) Mr. Sakei's.
(D) Mr. Pizzini's.

179. For what publication does Mr. Pizzini write?
(A) Downtown.
(B) Los Angeles Tribune.
(C) Bel-Air Journal of Design.
(D) Cutting Edge L.A.

180. Who is Ms. Leiber?
(A) A senior curator.
(B) A deputy director.
(C) An acclaimed artist.
(D) An art critic.

From:	thomas_foy@mailbox.com
To:	customerservice@lonestarsports.com
Re:	Purchase Order 4328
Date:	June 13

✉ T. Foy Bank Statement (PDF) 23.6k

Dear Customer Service,

On May 28, I purchased a pair of Maxx Shock Z28 running shoes at the Lone Star Sports' Arlington location. I paid for the purchase with my debit card. I have been pleased with the shoes and was satisfied with the price and the quality of the item.

When I received my bank statement, however, I noticed that I had been charged twice. I called the Arlington store to resolve the problem. The clerk said that there was a company-wide system problem that day, which resulted in several duplicate charges. She told me to e-mail customer service, and a representative would promptly <u>handle</u> the issue and reimburse me accordingly.

I have attached my bank statement for your reference.

Sincerely,
Thomas Foy

GO ON TO THE NEXT PAGE.

Statement

A Division of Texas
Commercial Finance Corp.

Date: June 1
STATEMENT # 98421

COMMENTS Statement period: May 1 – May 30

BILL
TO

Thomas Foy
2389 Walkerton Street,
Dallas, Texas 54383
Customer ID FNB92232

Date	Description	Balance	Amount
May 5	Electronic Salary Transfer - Jersey Construction Co.	$16,829.01	+$7,023.33
May 11	Derby Market, Dallas, TX	$16,794.36	-$34.65
May 15	Fort Worth Florist, Ft. Worth, TX	$16,694.36	-$100.00
May 16	Derby Market, Dallas, TX	$16,459.39	-$234.97
May 28	Lone Star Sports, Arlington, TX	$16,337.72	-$121.67
May 28	Lone Star Sports, Arlington, TC	$16,216.05	-$121.67

Current	1-30 Days Past Due	31-60 Days Past Due	61-90 Days Past Due	Over 90 Days Past Due	Ending balance
n/a	n/a	n/a	n/a		$16,216.05

CONTACT US AT FNBTX.COM
Thank you for your business!

181. In the e-mail, the word "handle" is closest in meaning to
(A) create.
(B) deliver.
(C) manage.
(D) hold.

182. When did Mr. Foy probably purchase flowers?
(A) On May 5.
(B) On May 11.
(C) On May 15.
(D) On May 28.

183. For what type of company does Mr. Foy most likely work?
(A) A construction company.
(B) A law firm.
(C) A local bank.
(D) A furniture store.

184. What does the e-mail indicate about Mr. Foy?
(A) He likes the shoes he purchased.
(B) He has visited the Arlington location several times since February.
(C) He is not pleased with the return policy at Lone Star Sports.
(D) He is a long-distance runner.

185. What amount does Mr. Foy expect to be refunded?
(A) $34.65.
(B) $100.00.
(C) $121.67.
(D) $234.97.

From:	Katrina Cline <kcline@russiantearoom.com>
To:	Chad Loomer <jloomer@russiantearoom.com>
Re:	Latest Update
Date:	July 17

Hello Chad,

My father just called to inform me that he has decided to have the restaurant renovated. As the on-site management team, the two of us will be the points of contact for the workers who will complete the project.

As a first step, I would like to ask you to identify some potential companies to do the work. Please begin looking into this as soon as possible and provide me with an update by July 31.

From:	Buddy Covington <bcovington@csrdesign.com>
To:	Katrina Cline <kcline@russiantearoom.com>
Re:	Project
Date:	August 7

Dear Ms. Cline,

On behalf of the team at Covington & Sons Restaurant Design, we are pleased that we have been selected for the Russian Tea Room's remodeling project. As I discussed with your assistant by telephone yesterday, we will provide a project supervisor and a designer who will be devoted to helping you create just the right look for your restaurant. We work with local wholesalers to offer you a wide selection of products, including paint, furniture, light fixtures and flooring, all within the restaurant's budget. We expect to complete the project by September 1.

We can discuss this information in more detail at our meeting on August 14.

Sincerely,
Buddy Covington
Covington and Sons Restaurant Design

GO ON TO THE NEXT PAGE.

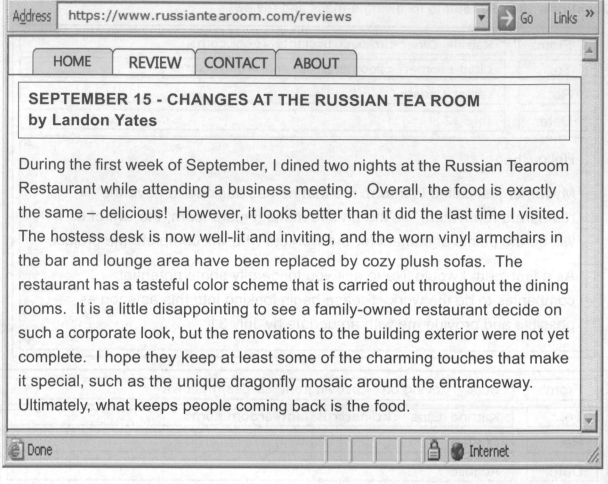

Address https://www.russiantearoom.com/reviews ▼ → Go Links »

| HOME | REVIEW | CONTACT | ABOUT |

SEPTEMBER 15 - CHANGES AT THE RUSSIAN TEA ROOM
by Landon Yates

During the first week of September, I dined two nights at the Russian Tearoom Restaurant while attending a business meeting. Overall, the food is exactly the same – delicious! However, it looks better than it did the last time I visited. The hostess desk is now well-lit and inviting, and the worn vinyl armchairs in the bar and lounge area have been replaced by cozy plush sofas. The restaurant has a tasteful color scheme that is carried out throughout the dining rooms. It is a little disappointing to see a family-owned restaurant decide on such a corporate look, but the renovations to the building exterior were not yet complete. I hope they keep at least some of the charming touches that make it special, such as the unique dragonfly mosaic around the entranceway. Ultimately, what keeps people coming back is the food.

Done 🔒 ⦿ Internet

186. Why was first e-mail sent?
(A) To announce a merger.
(B) To offer a suggestion.
(C) To assign a task.
(D) To update a schedule.

187. What is Mr. Yates unhappy about?
(A) The bar lounge furniture is uncomfortable.
(B) The reception area is too brightly lit.
(C) The restaurant has lost some of its charm.
(D) The restaurant was bought by a large corporation.

188. Who most likely did Mr. Covington talk to on August 6?
(A) Mr. Loomer.
(B) Mr. Yates.
(C) Ms. Cline.
(D) Mr. Cline.

189. What is suggested about the renovation?
(A) It cost more than anticipated.
(B) It included the addition of meeting rooms.
(C) It has caused an increase in reservations.
(D) It was not completed on schedule.

190. What does Mr. Covington offer Ms. Cline in his e-mail to her?
(A) To make decisions rapidly with the vendors.
(B) To provide dedicated staff members for the project.
(C) To send her weekly memos on the status of the project.
(D) To pay a penalty if the project is finished late.

SUSCA Spencer University School of Culinary Arts

808 Edgewater Boulevard - Gaithersburg, Maryland 24977

Register now for classes designed to help you develop cutting-edge food preparation and hospitality skills. All classes are taught by instructors with extensive professional experience and meet for fifteen weeks starting in either the second week of February or in the second week of September.

BASIC KITCHEN ACCOUNTING

Instructor: Arlene Raphael

Sharpen your administration skills by managing inventory, food costs, and labor expenses.

Meeting times: Monday and Wednesday, 7:15—9:00 P.M.

PROFESSIONAL DINING SERVICE

Instructor: Takeshi Harada

Learn the basic components and structure of dining service rules and etiquette.

Meeting time: Tuesday, 7:15—9:00 P.M.

FOOD SANITATION ESSENTIALS

Instructor: Cameron Vegas

Learn the proper food handling and storage techniques, as well as government regulations

Meeting time: Thursday, 7:15—9:00 P.M.

BAKING BASICS

Instructor: N'dela Odimpi

Take your cooking skills to the next level by learning how to bake.

Meeting times: Friday, 7:15—9:30 P.M.

Note: Classes may be taken individually or bundled. The American Culinary Certification (Level II) requires participants to successfully complete all four classes in the program.

GO ON TO THE NEXT PAGE.

From:	bmxavier@scootmail.com
To:	araphael@susca.edu
Re:	Job Reference
Date:	November 4

✉ Xavier resume and job description (PDF) 23.6K

Dear Ms. Raphael,

I am applying for a position at Ida's Jack Steakhouse and would like to know if I may use you as a reference since your class was most relevant to the job. Please let me know at your earliest convenience. I would like to submit my application by the end of this week and need to include my references in the online application. I have attached a document for you to review, it includes both the job description and my resume.

Thank you again for your instruction. I enjoyed being in your class.

Barry Monroe Xavier

From:	araphael@susca.edu
To:	bmxavier@scootmail.com
Re:	Job Reference
Date:	November 4

Hi Mr. Xavier,

I would be happy to serve as a reference. You picked up the information presented in our class very quickly, so I think you'll be a good fit for a fast-paced environment like Ida's Jack. I reviewed your resume and just wanted to remind you that the class was one that contributes to a certificate. You completed the program in June, so you should indicate that you earned a Level II ACF certification.

Best wishes!
Arlene Raphael, SUSCA Instructor

191. What is stated about all of the listed classes?
(A) They are designed specifically for restaurant owners.
(B) They are offered twice a year.
(C) They must be taken together.
(D) They focus on how to start a business.

192. What is suggested about Mr. Xavier?
(A) He is a candidate for a job at SUSCA.
(B) He failed Ms. Raphael's class.
(C) He completed four classes at SUSCA.
(D) He earned a certificate in April.

193. What about Mr. Xavier most impressed Ms. Raphael?
(A) His resume.
(B) His certifications.
(C) His learning speed.
(D) His test scores.

194. Who most likely has experience in a bakery?
(A) Mr. Vegas.
(B) Ms. Odimpi.
(C) Ms. Raphael.
(D) Mr. Harada.

195. What type of position is Mr. Xavier probably interviewing for?
(A) Pastry chef.
(B) Restaurant manager.
(C) Business writer.
(D) Bartender's assistant.

GO ON TO THE NEXT PAGE.

City of Tempe

Requests to Film on City Property

Permits for filming on city property are issued by the Tempe Department of Public Works. Application documents should be completed online at least two weeks in advance of the proposed filming date(s) to allow adequate time for review. Read the following carefully before completing the application.

- Fill in every portion of the form. If not applicable, write "N/A".

- Describe each location and exactly what you plan to film there. Be specific.

- All production companies must pay a nonrefundable application fee of $500.

- Charitable organizations or individuals working on private projects are charged an application fee of $250.

- If amplified sound is used, proof of a noise permit will be required.

- If filming impedes pedestrians' ability to use a sidewalk, a traffic-control officer must be hired at the applicant's expense.

Application for Filming Permit

Applicant information

Name	Address
Rino Pescatore	1780 E University Ave, Tempe, AZ 88003

Phone	Company
554-1393	Name n/a

Purpose of Filming and Summary of Activities:

I am an undergraduate filmmaker at Arizona State University, and this is part of my final project. My crew will be filming two scenes at Apodaca Park: one scene in the garden behind the Mesilla Valley Polo Club, and one scene that will involve actors chasing each other on the sidewalk along Mesilla Valley Drive at the Apodaca Boathouse. We will have handheld cameras, a tripod, three vehicles, and minimal lighting equipment, but no sound equipment. Our only props will be an umbrella, a hockey stick, and a shovel.

Filming Schedule:

Date	Location	Start/End Times	Number of Cast/Crew
April 9	Polo Club garden	8:00 A.M.—Noon	3-7 people
April 10	Mesilla Valley Drive at Apodaca Boathouse	8:00 A.M.—Noon	3-10 people

GO ON TO THE NEXT PAGE.

City of Tempe

Special Use Permit #002-0214

Rino Pescatore   of   1780 E University Ave, Tempe, AZ 88003
(Name of Permittee)   (Address)

is hereby authorized to use Apodaca Park during the period of April 9 — April 10 between the hours of 8:00 a.m. and 10:30 a.m. for the purpose of a university film project.

Specific locations: Polo Club Garden and Mesilla Valley Drive at Apodaca Boathouse
Maximum number of people: 10   **Maximum number of vehicles:** 3
Permittee Signature: *Rino Pescatore*   **Print Name:** Rino Pescatore
Authorizing Official Signature: *Mona Jarvis*   **Print Name:** Mona Jarvis

Please note: This permit must be **displayed** at all times while on location. Violation of the conditions state above will result in the permit being revoked.

---

196. What do the instructions indicate about the Tempe Department of Public Works?
(A) It requires more than one week to process permit applications.
(B) It issues more permits to individuals than to production companies.
(C) It recommends that applications be submitted by postal mail.
(D) It recently set limits on the number of permits issued per month.

197. What request of Mr. Pescatore was only partly allowed?
(A) The size of the group that he hoped could participate.
(B) The number of locations that he wished to use.
(C) The amount of time that he wanted to be on-site.
(D) The amount of equipment that be wanted to bring.

198. What is Mr. Pescatore required to do with his permit?
(A) E-mail it to the park managers.
(B) Post it at each filming location.
(C) Keep it on file at his university.
(D) Submit it to his insurer.

199. What is mentioned in the instructions about the city's permit applications fees?
(A) They differ according to the location being filmed.
(B) They will be returned if the permit is not issued.
(C) They can be paid in monthly installments.
(D) They are reduced for certain applicants.

200. What is implied about Mr. Pescatore?
(A) He has a special noise permit.
(B) He will be visited by a city inspector.
(C) He will need traffic-control assistance.
(D) He is an employee of a university.

Stop! This is the end of the test. If you finish before time is called, you may go back to Parts 5, 6, and 7 and check your work.

New TOEIC Listening Script

PART 1

1. (   ) (A) The men are painting the side of a warehouse.
        (B) The men are pushing a cart down the road.
        (C) The men are watching television and having a beer.
        (D) The men are wearing hard hats and safety vests.

2. (   ) (A) The woman is drinking tea.
        (B) The cashier is standing next to the cash register.
        (C) The customer is looking through her purse.
        (D) The man is talking on a cell phone.

3. (   ) (A) The workers are cleaning up a beach.
        (B) The workers are cutting down a tree.
        (C) The workers are taking down a scaffold.
        (D) The workers are repairing a road.

4. (   ) (A) Some kids are playing a game.
        (B) Some people are at a park.
        (C) The host is offering beverages.
        (D) The performer is pointing at someone in the audience.

5. (   ) (A) The boy is playing with a toy.
        (B) The girl is not wearing her seatbelt.
        (C) The man is learning how to drive a truck.
        (D) The woman is riding a bicycle.

6. (   ) (A) The saxophone is on a shelf.
        (B) The piano is in the middle of the room.
        (C) The drums are in the alley.
        (D) The guitar is in a glass case.

GO ON TO THE NEXT PAGE.

PART 2

7. (   ) When do you think we'll hear if we've won the Lees account?
   (A) No, we haven't found one yet.
   (B) Because I was out of town.
   (C) Mr. Winston might already know.

8. (   ) Didn't Mr. Swisher accept the job offer?
   (A) He'll let us know tomorrow.
   (B) At the board meeting next Tuesday.
   (C) The sales department.

9. (   ) How will I know if the basketball game is canceled?
   (A) Have you been checked-in?
   (B) You could look on the team's Web site.
   (C) These seats are empty.

10. (   ) How many tables did you reserve?
    (A) No, not right now.
    (B) Eight of them.
    (C) Around the corner from the office.

11. (   ) Have you opened the front entrance yet?
    (A) Open a customer account.
    (B) No—I don't have a key.
    (C) It is a 10-minute walk from here.

12. (   ) What time is the board meeting?
    (A) In the main conference room.
    (B) Her name is Susanne.
    (C) It starts at 1:30.

13. (   ) Where should I put these binders for the sales presentation?
    (A) Almost everyone signed up.
    (B) On the table by the door.
    (C) Just coffee, tea, and some pastries.

14. (   ) I don't know which computer model to buy?
    (A) Because it's running low on battery.
    (B) What features are most important to you?
    (C) A shop in the mall.

15. (   ) Who has the combination to the safe?
    (A) $500 a piece.
    (B) Your supervisor should know it.
    (C) The alarm system works well.

16. (   ) Who's responsible for making hiring decisions?
    (A) The personnel director usually handles that.
    (B) If I have time.
    (C) Salaries are based on education and work experience.

17. (   ) What's the charge to go to the hotel?
    (A) It'll cost you thirty dollars.
    (B) It needs a new handle.
    (C) You should allow half an hour.

18. (   ) Which model gets the most kilometers to the liter?
    (A) About an hour's drive at the most.
    (B) The smaller one is extremely efficient.
    (C) It's a 10-kilometer race.

19. (   ) When does the European Trade Conference take place?
    (A) During the third week of September.
    (B) Last winter in Brussels.
    (C) Since Tuesday.

20. (   ) What do you think of the new reception area?
    (A) It's a definite improvement.
    (B) She seems very well qualified.
    (C) I haven't received it yet.

21. (   ) When will the staff be moving to the new building?
    (A) Yes, a month ago.
    (B) In about two weeks.
    (C) For several hours.

22. (   ) What does Miss Roberts do professionally?
    (A) She works in a law firm.
    (B) She doesn't think so.
    (C) She's talking to the professor.

GO ON TO THE NEXT PAGE.

23. (　　) Which division earned the most money last quarter?
    (A) For the next year's marketing budget.
    (B) By cutting the salary.
    (C) The Canadian sales office.

24. (　　) When did you speak with Mr. Field?
    (A) Because it was important.
    (B) I believe it was late last week.
    (C) When he gets back to the office.

25. (　　) When will the opening in the legal division be filled?
    (A) By advertising on the Internet.
    (B) When Miss Junko returns from vacation.
    (C) A good position for a legal assistant.

26. (　　) When did the labor dispute reach a resolution?
    (A) We should get there by lunchtime.
    (B) The issue was settled late last night.
    (C) Yes, everyone seemed to agree on the terms.

27. (　　) Who's going to replace Mr. Park?
    (A) Someone from the regional office.
    (B) Please return it to the clerk.
    (C) He doesn't want to travel so much.

28. (　　) Who is going to move into the offices on the third floor?
    (A) A small law firm has just signed a lease.
    (B) Not more than five.
    (C) Almost 50 euros per square foot.

29. (　　) Where is the baggage claim area?
    (A) Not without your receipt.
    (B) Go straight down to the first floor.
    (C) No, I have two large suitcases.

30. (　　) Where can I get a replacement filter for this air-conditioner?
    (A) By the end of the month.
    (B) Yes, fill it up to the top.
    (C) Order one from the catalogue.

31. (   ) Why aren't any of the computer terminals turned on?
    (A) The new hardware system is being installed this morning.
    (B) Yes, I turned them on when I arrived today.
    (C) Because this bus terminal is always so busy.

PART 3

Questions 32 through 34 *refer to the following conversation.*

M : Hello, I'm calling about a door I'm repairing for you. I wanted to order the exact same door knob to replace the one that's missing, but it is no longer available. So you have to choose a different one.

W : That's OK. I remember seeing a door knob in your shop that I like. It's round and silver and found on display in your front window. Do you think you could use that instead?

M : Sure, but I will have to order one because I don't have another one in stock. So the repair won't be done for another two weeks.

32. (   ) Why is the man calling the woman?
    (A) To discuss a consultation.
    (B) To provide a business address.
    (C) To promote new service.
    (D) To discuss a repair.

33. (   ) What does the woman describe?
    (A) Some window designs.
    (B) A room arrangement.
    (C) A paint color.
    (D) A door knob.

34. (   ) What does the man say he has to do?
    (A) Order some items.
    (B) Extend a warranty.
    (C) Offer a discount.
    (D) Mail some samples.

Questions 35 through 37 *refer to the following conversation.*

M : Dina, have you seen our sales figures? We sold a lot fewer travel guides and cookbooks last quarter. And overall, our profits are down 17 percent.

GO ON TO THE NEXT PAGE.

W : Foot traffic has been down in all our locations. I don't know if that's a reflection of the economy or what.

M : I've been saying this for a long time, but we need to start selling books from our Web site.

W : Well, Tim, we agreed at the beginning of this venture that we would not get into online commerce, and I think we need to stick with our brick-and-mortar business model.

35. (   ) Who most likely are the speakers?
   (A) Authors.
   (B) Magazine editors.
   (C) Software developers.
   (D) Bookstore owners.

36. (   ) What does the man suggest doing?
   (A) Drafting an article for a magazine.
   (B) Rescheduling a product launch.
   (C) Selling products on the Internet.
   (D) Reviewing a publishing contract.

37. (   ) What does the woman object to?
   (A) Ordering additional merchandise.
   (B) Opening another store.
   (C) Changing the business model.
   (D) Spending on advertisement.

Questions 38 through 40 _refer to the following conversation._

W : Hi, this is Yolanda Peters calling. I was in your office for a dental exam last week and ordered a new mouth guard. I was told to call back today to check whether it is ready.

M : Hello, Ms. Peters. We will have it ready for you later today. You can come in any time after two o'clock to pick it up.

W : Okay, great. I can stop by before you close. Could you tell me how the discount coupon works? I received one when I had my teeth cleaned here last time. Can I use it for this purchase?

M : Yes, since the cost of this order is over one hundred dollars. You can use it to get 50% off the total price. Just present the coupon when you pay.

38. (   ) Why is the woman calling?
   (A) To get driving directions.
   (B) To inquire about a job.
   (C) To make an appointment.
   (D) To check on an order.

39. (　　) What does the woman say she will do?
  - (A) Call her insurance company.
  - (B) Consult another doctor.
  - (C) Send an application.
  - (D) Visit an office.

40. (　　) What does the man explain?
  - (A) How to receive a discount.
  - (B) How to obtain medical records.
  - (C) How to repair an item.
  - (D) How to check an account status.

Questions 41 through 43 *refer to the following conversation.*

W : Hi, I'd like to submit this application for a Chinese business visa. I'm hoping to leave for Shanghai next week.

M : Well, I suggest you pay for the expedited service. We will process your application today. And you can come back to pick up your business visa tomorrow.

W : That's great. I will be able to take my trip then. Do I pay you for that faster service?

M : No, you need to go to window 10 to pay the processing fee. Only cash or credit cards are accepted.

41. (　　) What is the woman trying to do?
  - (A) Book a hotel.
  - (B) Apply for a visa.
  - (C) Open an account.
  - (D) Send a package.

42. (　　) What does the man recommend?
  - (A) Reading some instructions.
  - (B) Requesting a receipt.
  - (C) Using a faster service.
  - (D) Choosing a different date.

43. (　　) What can the woman do at window 10?
  - (A) Speak to a supervisor.
  - (B) Receive a voucher.
  - (C) Have her photograph taken.
  - (D) Pay a fee.

GO ON TO THE NEXT PAGE.

Questions 44 through 46 *refer to the following conversation.*

W : Grant? It's Rebecca. I've just missed my flight back to Nashville. I'll have to spend another night in L.A., and I'm booked on another 3:00 p.m. flight, so I won't make it into the office tomorrow.

M : Hmm, I was counting on you being here tomorrow at 9:00 a.m. for an important meeting. Do you think you could arrange to meet through a video-conferencing?

W : Well, there is a business center here in the hotel. But I'm not sure if it's equipped for video-conferencing. Let me go down there and see if the center has the necessary equipment.

44. (   ) What problem does the woman inform the man about?
        (A) She lost her computer.
        (B) Her luggage did not arrive.
        (C) Her password is incorrect.
        (D) She missed a flight.

45. (   ) What does the man suggest?
        (A) Consulting a travel agency.
        (B) Using a car service to visit a client.
        (C) Joining a meeting by video-conference.
        (D) Returning to a hotel.

46. (   ) What does the woman plan to do next?
        (A) Check for some equipment.
        (B) Call an airline.
        (C) Report a complaint.
        (D) Go to a repair shop.

Questions 47 through 49 *refer to the following conversation with three speakers.*

Woman UK : Hey, guys. I need a minute with you because I'm writing up the new employee training manual we'll be discussing at tomorrow's meeting.

Man Canada : Oh, hi, Laura. I got an e-mail this morning saying that the meeting has been rescheduled for next week.

Man Aus : Yeah, me too.

Woman UK : That's news to me. I'll get a hold of Brad Palmer and see what that's about, but the training manual remains a pressing concern. So, I'd like to get some feedback and suggestions from both of you.

Man Canada : Well, I'm really jammed for time this morning, since I have a deadline on the contract for the recycling project.

Woman UK : How about you, George?

Man Aus : I'm dealing with a backlog of orders in the warehouse. But if you give me the draft, I will be happy to take a look at it right after lunch.

47. (   ) What is the woman preparing?
   (A) Some order forms.
   (B) Some training materials.
   (C) A meeting agenda.
   (D) An office newsletter.

48. (   ) Why did the woman say, "That's news to me"?
   (A) She had already booked a conference room.
   (B) She thought a delivery had been made.
   (C) She was unaware that a meeting had been postponed.
   (D) She believed that policy had changed.

49. (   ) What does George agree to do after lunch?
   (A) Sign an agreement.
   (B) Review a document.
   (C) Confirm a deadline.
   (D) Email a colleague.

Questions 50 through 52 refer to the following conversation between three speakers.

Man : Our clothes are selling really well, so the company has decided to expand our market into Latin America and sell our product line there, too. They're hiring a new regional manager. Do either of you have any interest in the job?

Woman UK : I might, but do you know any details about the job?

Man : Well, the job posting says retail stores will be opening in Panama, Brazil, and possibly other countries later on. They are looking for someone to oversee the operation of the new stores. Don't you speak Spanish, Paula?

Woman US : Yes, I speak decent Spanish and have spent time in Latin America, so I would probably be an asset in working with the staff there. I may be qualified.

Man : That's great! How about you, Wendy? Any interest in the job?

Woman UK : I don't speak a foreign language and I've never traveled abroad, so it might not be a good fit for me.

GO ON TO THE NEXT PAGE.

50. (   ) What type of company do the speakers work for?
    (A) A travel agency.
    (B) A furniture manufacturer.
    (C) An interior design firm.
    (D) A clothing retailer.

51. (   ) According to the man, what is the main responsibility of the position?
    (A) Supervising an assembly line.
    (B) Developing a sales strategy.
    (C) Managing multiple stores.
    (D) Creating product designs.

52. (   ) What qualification does Paula mention?
    (A) She has a large number of clients.
    (B) She speaks a foreign language.
    (C) She is familiar with the company's products.
    (D) She is an expert in retail trends

Questions 53 through 55 _refer to the following conversation._

M : So, how was the meeting with the designers? I'm dying to know what you think of the new autumn clothing line.

W : Well, I'm wearing a pair of the leggings. They're made of 95 percent cotton and 5 percent polyester, and they're really quite comfortable.

M : That's a great selling point! Let's make comfort the central focus of our advertising campaign.

53. (   ) What industry do the speakers most likely work in?
    (A) Advertising.
    (B) Energy.
    (C) Tourism.
    (D) Fashion.

54. (   ) What does the woman say about a new product?
    (A) It is comfortable.
    (B) It is inexpensive.
    (C) It is selling well.
    (D) It is being redesigned.

55. (   ) What does the man suggest?
(A) Arranging a press conference.
(B) Promoting a special feature.
(C) Initiating product testing.
(D) Giving away free samples.

Questions 56 through 58 refer to the following conversation.

W : I'm excited to about Lathrop's plan to bring in more customers. I've seen the upcoming ad campaign, and I think it will be really effective in attracting new business.

M : Yes, I agree, as long as we schedule to run print ads in June issues of selected magazines.

W : Right, and we launch the television ad campaign after that in July. But I hear there are still some discussions about whether to focus the television ads on Internet banking or home loans.

M : I think that Internet banking would appeal more to the type of customers we are looking for. And on television, they are really able to visualize all the features of the system.

56. (   ) What are the speakers mainly discussing?
(A) The announcement of a new manager.
(B) The introduction of a special service.
(C) Plans for increasing business.
(D) Procedures for a departmental process.

57. (   ) What will happen in July?
(A) Television advertisements will be launched.
(B) Client testimonials will be posted online.
(C) A new Internet bank will be established.
(D) An advertising agency will be hired.

58. (   ) What does the man say will appeal to customers?
(A) Foreign currency exchange.
(B) Extended business hours.
(C) Home loans.
(D) Online banking.

Questions 59 through 61 refer to the following conversation.

M : Welcome back to the Business Network, I'm your host, Jack Lee. In our studio today, Sophia Rizzo, president and CEO of Quasar Motors, is here to discuss her company's new eco-friendly car. Sophia, what can you tell us about your new product?

GO ON TO THE NEXT PAGE.

W : Our new car, the Oasia, will be the first vehicle to run solely on compressed air. This technology has been around for many years, but this is the first car that doesn't also use gasoline or electricity for fuel.

M : You're kidding! That's amazing. So how far along are you in the production process? When will the car be available?

W : The final testing of the pre-production models will be completed in a few months. So expect that 6 months from now, the first Oasia will be on the market.

59. (   ) Who is Sophia Rizzo?
    (A) A television producer.
    (B) A car company president.
    (C) An aircraft designer.
    (D) An electrical engineer.

60. (   ) Why does the man say, "You're kidding!"?
    (A) He strongly disagrees.
    (B) He would like an explanation.
    (C) He feels disappointed.
    (D) He is happily surprised.

61. (   ) According to the woman, what will happen in six months?
    (A) A vehicle will be available for purchase.
    (B) A new television series will begin.
    (C) A business update will be published.
    (D) Production costs will increase.

Questions 62 through 64 refer to the following conversation and list of passengers.

W : Hi, I'm one of the names listed on your sign. Tara Crover, with Goldstar Incorporated. I'm here for the electronics convention. I take it you're going to drive us to the hotel. Have any of my colleagues arrived yet?

M : Welcome to San Francisco, Ms. Crover. You're the first to arrive. I believe your associate from Chicago is due to arrive shortly. Unfortunately, your colleagues coming from Atlanta have been delayed. Their flight was re-routed through Pittsburgh.

W : When are they expected to arrive?

M : Not until 8:30 this evening.

W : Um, we'll miss the opening reception if we wait for them.

M : We won't. We'll only wait for your colleague coming from Chicago. I'll drive the two of you to the hotel and then return for the others. Here——let me take your bag to the waiting area.

62. (   ) What is the purpose of the woman's trip?
   (A) To negotiate a contract.
   (B) To visit family.
   (C) To attend a trade show.
   (D) To interview for a job.

63. (   ) Look at the graphic. Who will arrive next?
   (A) Alan Wurtz.
   (B) Hope Dane-Wallace.
   (C) Tara Crover.
   (D) Francisco De La Rosa.

SAROVAR HOTELS & RESORTS	GOLDSTAR INC.	
Name		**Departure City**
Mr. Alan Wurtz		Atlanta
Ms. Hope Dane-Wallace		Atlanta
Ms. Tara Crover		Denver
Mr. Francisco De La Rosa		Chicago

64. (   ) What does the man offer to do for the woman?
   (A) Pay a fee.
   (B) Buy some coffee.
   (C) Carry her luggage.
   (D) Give her a massage.

Questions 65 through 67 refer to the following conversation and bulletin board posting.

W : Hi, I'm calling about a post on the community bulletin board indicating you're selling a
    camping tent. Could you tell me more about it?
M : Sure, it's a Moleman 6-Person Weather Chief. Six by 15 feet. Aqua blue in color. I'm only
    asking a hundred for it. Do you want to come and have a look at it?
W : I would but I'm on my way out of town for a few days. Can you e-mail some pictures? If I
    like it, I can stop by and pick it up on the way home from my trip.
M : I can do that. I'll send it to you shortly. What's your e-mail address?

GO ON TO THE NEXT PAGE.

65. (   ) Why is the woman calling?
    (A) To inquire about an item.
    (B) To cancel a purchase.
    (C) To report a lost item.
    (D) To get driving directions.

66. (   ) Look at the graphic? Who is the woman speaking with?
    (A) John Moss.
    (B) Vicki Wang.
    (C) Fred Gustavson.
    (D) Beth Grant.

BROOKFIELD COMMUNITY BULLETIN BOARD
WANTED: Used clothing, books, appliances - please call John Moss at St. Mark's Mission (202) 434-9090
Piano Lessons - Group or private - Best rates - Vicki Wang (202) 213-3444
For Sale: Kommander Weather Chief 6-Person Camping Tent. 6' x 15' - $100 - Good condition. Call Fred Gustavson (202) 213-0771
Volunteer Abroad! Many fulfilling opportunities with Frontier Foundation. (202) 434-2332. Call now! Ask for Beth Grant

67. (   ) What does the man say he will e-mail?
    (A) An itinerary.
    (B) A contract.
    (C) Some instructions.
    (D) Some images.

Questions 68 through 70 *refer to the following conversation and guide.*

M : Hello, this is my first visit to your café. Can you recommend a coffee drink for me?

W : Sure, what kind of coffee do you usually enjoy? Latte? Cappuccino? Americano?

M : I've only ever had regular brewed coffee. But my co-worker told me that you make some really tasty drinks. So I think I'd like to try something new. Do you make anything with chocolate?

W : We sure do! We have several options, but I'd recommend the café mocha. We're actually having a promotion on our specialty drinks. If you buy one, you'll get half off your next purchase.

M : Great, I'd like to try one. Does it cost the same as the other drinks?

W : It's not our most expensive item. Here's a price list for you.

68. (   ) Why does the man want to try a new drink?
    (A) It was recommended by a co-worker.
    (B) It was featured in a news report.
    (C) He's on a diet.
    (D) It has health benefits.

69. (   ) What will the man receive with his purchase?
    (A) A pastry.
    (B) A membership card.
    (C) A discount on his next purchase.
    (D) A gift certificate.

70. (   ) Look at the graphic. How much did the man pay for his drink?
    (A) 2.50.
    (B) 3.00.
    (C) 3.50.
    (D) 4.00.

Beverage	Price
Latte	2.50
Cappuccino	3.00
Café Mocha	3.50
Café Miel	4.00

GO ON TO THE NEXT PAGE.

PART 4

Questions 71 through 73 *refer to the following announcement.*

Welcome aboard this afternoon's Jet King flight 5J311 non-stop to Little Rock. While we taxi to the runway, I'd like to tell you about a new service offered by Jet King Airlines. In addition to movies and music, you can now access digital versions of a wide variety of magazines from the entertainment module on the seat-back in front of you. You'll be able to read current and previous issues of a range of magazines using the touchscreen monitor. If you'd like to use this service, just swipe your credit card to get started.

71. (   ) Where is the announcement being made?
      (A) On an airplane.
      (B) On a tour bus.
      (C) At a bank.
      (D) At a theater.

72. (   ) What service is the speaker mainly explaining?
      (A) Personal concierge.
      (B) Digital entertainment.
      (C) Food options.
      (D) Discount tickets.

73. (   ) What does the speaker say the listeners should do to use a service?
      (A) Open an account.
      (B) Sign up in advance.
      (C) Download a mobile app.
      (D) Enter credit card information.

Questions 74 through 76 *refer to the following broadcast.*

You're listening to 'Access Houston'——the podcast for entrepreneurs and small business owners in Houston. One thing all business owners big or small need is good accounting software to keep track of their inventory. Today I'll be reviewing a few accounting software programs that I've worked with over the years, but right now I want to remind you that this podcast is made possible by the generous support of our sponsor, Wizard Solutions. If you're in the market for affordable and reliable Web hosting, visit the Wizard Solutions Web site for the latest promotional deals.

74. (   ) Who is the intended audience of the podcast?
  (A) Small business owners.
  (B) Corporate trainers.
  (C) Civil engineers.
  (D) Health-care professionals.

75. (   ) What will the speaker discuss on today's show?
  (A) Leadership skills.
  (B) Real Estate.
  (C) Accounting software.
  (D) Customer relations.

76. (   ) What does the speaker suggest the listeners do?
  (A) Enter a contest.
  (B) Visit a Web site.
  (C) Submit their questions.
  (D) Attend an event.

Questions 77 through 79 *refer to the following instructions.*

Good morning! My name is Rick and I'm the maintenance foreman at our factory.
Our new sheet metal cutting equipment was installed by technicians last night. These
machines can cut up to 10 layers of sheet metal at once, which will make all of your
jobs a little easier and expedite the process on the factory production line. For optimal
results, the gears of each machine will need to be cleaned every day——ideally, at the
beginning of each shift. I've posted a maintenance schedule at each cutting station.
Now, if someone will use the dolly to roll that bolt of steel over here, I'll demonstrate
how these machines work.

77. (   ) Where does the talk most likely take place?
  (A) At a trade show.
  (B) At a dry-cleaning store.
  (C) At a factory.
  (D) At a repair shop.

78. (   ) What are the listeners advised to do every day?
  (A) Use industrial earplugs.
  (B) Take inventory.
  (C) Meet production quotas.
  (D) Clean some equipment.

GO ON TO THE NEXT PAGE.

79. (　　) What does the speaker say he will do next?
    (A) Give a demonstration.
    (B) Distribute a questionnaire.
    (C) Introduce a visitor.
    (D) Take a short break.

Questions 80 through 82 _refer to the following talk._

Hey guys. I appreciate everybody being on time for the staff meeting. To kick things off, I have the honor of awarding the Salesperson of the Month to Harrison Camp. Harrison's been leading our business-to-business division for three years now, and most recently worked on our social media campaign. Harrison was responsible for increasing our company's visibility by posting ads on popular sites. Thanks to his work, in the past month we've generated 15% more sales leads from people signing up for our email newsletter. On top of that, next week Harrison will be leading an in-house seminar on marketing innovation. Please give a warm welcome to Harrison Camp, our Salesperson of the Month.

80. (　　) What is the purpose of the talk?
    (A) To welcome a new employee.
    (B) To celebrate a corporate merger.
    (C) To remind staff of a policy.
    (D) To announce an award winner.

81. (　　) What does the speaker say has recently increased?
    (A) Local taxes.
    (B) Sales leads.
    (C) Quarterly travel spending.
    (D) Insurance deductibles.

82. (　　) What will Harrison Camp be doing next week?
    (A) Leading a seminar.
    (B) Launching a product.
    (C) Attending a convention.
    (D) Hiring an assistant.

Questions 83 through 85 *refer to the following telephone message.*

Hi Chelsea, it's Amelia. I'm calling about the new food processor model. As you know, we've scheduled the first round of consumer focus groups. While we're always concerned about having people review a model that's still in the development stage, keep in mind that we'll only be asking participants about the appearance of the food processor at this point. You can continue to work out the remaining details in terms of the interior electronics. Then, once your department is ready with a prototype, we'll definitely hold a second round of focus groups. Meanwhile, could you please let me know the date you think your team will be ready for the first round?

83. (   ) Where does the speaker most likely work?
(A) At a culinary academy.
(B) At an electronics manufacturer.
(C) At an advertising firm.
(D) At an appliance store.

84. (   ) Why does the speaker say, "We'll only be asking reviewers about the appearance of the food processor at this point"?
(A) To reassure the listener about a mutual concern.
(B) To show disappointment in a decision.
(C) To suggest a change in product design.
(D) To clarify that a deadline has passed.

85. (   ) What does the speaker ask the listener to do?
(A) Give a presentation.
(B) Design a prototype.
(C) Create an advertisement.
(D) Provide a date.

Questions 86 through 88 *refer to the following announcement.*

Attention shoppers. Head on over to the Bake Shop where you can sample our new line of delicious gluten-free bakery items. I understand Landon has just baked a fresh batch of oatmeal cookies. Our gluten-free recipes are more flavorful than other bakeries because there's nothing artificial added to the organic flour substitute we use. And this week only we're selling all gluten-free items at a 20 percent discount.

GO ON TO THE NEXT PAGE.

86. (   ) Where is the announcement being made?
    (A) In an airport.
    (B) At a job fair.
    (C) At a supermarket.
    (D) In a restaurant.

87. (   ) What does the speaker invite the listeners to do?
    (A) Pick up a coupon.
    (B) Get in a line.
    (C) Purchase a membership.
    (D) Try a sample.

88. (   ) According to the speaker, why do the bakery items taste better?
    (A) They are made with special equipment.
    (B) The beans are roasted locally.
    (C) They have no chemical additives.
    (D) They were imported from another country.

Questions 89 through 91 _refer to an excerpt from a meeting._

It shouldn't surprise any of us that our company's been facing stiff competition in recent months. Since our competitors have been establishing a strong presence in the market, in order to gain a competitive edge, it's essential that everyone in this department hone their marketing skills. So I scheduled a professional development workshop next Thursday at 2 o'clock. Some of you may have other meetings scheduled at that time, but this is important to our company's future. Following the seminar, I'll send you a form asking for your detailed feedback. Please be sure to complete it and send it to me within 24 hours after you receive it.

89. (   ) According to the speaker, what has happened in recent months?
    (A) Competition from other companies has increased.
    (B) Employees have reported low job satisfaction.
    (C) Manufacturing goals have not been met.
    (D) A product release has been delayed.

90. (   ) What should listeners send to the speaker?
    (A) A list of client contacts.
    (B) A feedback form.
    (C) A travel itinerary.
    (D) Expense reports.

91. (   ) What does the speaker imply when she says, "This is important to our company's future"?
    (A) She hopes to find an alternative solution.
    (B) She wants to recognize the listeners' efforts.
    (C) She wants to accommodate a client's request.
    (D) She expects employees to attend a seminar.

Questions 92 through 94 refer to the following tour information.

And this concludes our tour of the White Beach Observatory. I hope it's been both educational and entertaining. Before you leave today, why not stop by our gift shop? We have a large selection of T-shirts, postcards, and calendars. As a public institution, we're partially funded by the purchases you make. Also, you may be interested in learning more about our Young Astronomer programs. Our education specialist, Olivia, is at the front desk.

92. (   ) Who most likely is the speaker?
    (A) A tour guide.
    (B) A sales clerk.
    (C) A scientist.
    (D) A corporate executive.

93. (   ) What does the speaker suggest that the listeners do before leaving?
    (A) Apply for a membership.
    (B) Fill out a survey.
    (C) Watch a short film.
    (D) Go to a gift shop.

94. (   ) Why does the speaker say, "Our education specialist, Olivia, is at the front desk"?
    (A) To request volunteers.
    (B) To indicate where to get information.
    (C) To deny a visitor's request.
    (D) To explain why she must leave.

Questions 95 through 97 refer to the following advertisement and price list.

It's February and that means Baker's Furniture is hosting its annual sale, and right now our very popular dining room table is on sale for 75% off the original price!

GO ON TO THE NEXT PAGE.

This deal is valid for in-store purchases only. You can just pick it up from the store. All of the parts are included in one small box. Our customers love this dining room table because it can be assembled at home quickly and easily. Just log on to our Web site to access our simple assembly instructions. Don't miss out on this deal! Come visit us at Baker's Furniture today.

95. (   ) Look at the graphic. What is the sale price of the table being described?
    (A) $180.
    (B) $250.
    (C) $275.
    (D) $300.

Item	Original Price	Sale Price
Dining room table	$1,200	$300
Coffee table	$540	$180
Patio table	$1,000	$250
Kitchen table	$1,100	$275

96. (   ) According to the speaker, why do customers like the table?
    (A) It is hand-made.
    (B) It is available in many colors.
    (C) It is easy to assemble.
    (D) It is inexpensive.

97. (   ) What does the speaker say can be found on a Web site?
    (A) Some instructions.
    (B) Some recipes.
    (C) A warranty.
    (D) A coupon.

Questions 98 through 100 *refer to the following telephone message and weather report.*

Hey Lindsey, this is Dylan. I'm calling about the music festival we've been planning to help raise funds for breast cancer awareness. Got a problem here, Lindsey. Have you seen the weather forecast? Apparently, it's supposed to be unseasonably hot on the day we were planning to hold our event. Over 112 degrees. Even with the use of industrial fans on stage, none of the performers will want to play under those conditions. So, I'd like you to get the team together tomorrow sometime to get things in order for an alternate date. Could you organize that? It's mostly minor planning adjustments that we'll need to make.

98. (　　) What event is being discussed?
   (A) A grand opening.
   (B) A charity walk.
   (C) A trip to the zoo.
   (D) A music festival.

99. (　　) Look at the graphic. Which day was the event originally scheduled for?
   (A) Thursday.
   (B) Friday.
   (C) Saturday.
   (D) Sunday.

Weather Forecast			
Thursday	Friday	Saturday	Sunday
Cloudy and humid	Light rain with scattered thunderstorms	Extreme heat	Sunny with onshore winds
High: 85 Low: 75	High: 90 Low: 80	High: 112+ Low: 88	High: 92 Low: 81

100. (　　) What does the speaker ask the listener to do?
   (A) Arrange a meeting.
   (B) Contact scheduled performers.
   (C) Rent industrial fans.
   (D) Print new tickets.

GO ON TO THE NEXT PAGE.

NO TEST MATERIAL ON THIS PAGE

New TOEIC Speaking Test

Question 1: Read a Text Aloud

 **Question 1**

Directions: In this part of the test, you will read aloud the text on the screen. You will have 45 seconds to prepare. Then you will have 45 seconds to read the text aloud.

The main point of this staff meeting is to inform you of some developments here at the department store in preparation for the start of the holiday season. We've moved our discounted items toward the front of the store to make room for the seasonal products that will soon begin arriving for display. And speaking of the holiday season, I know a lot of you will be looking to take time off to spend with your families. So, I have posted a vacation request sign-up sheet outside the management office. I can't guarantee every request will be filled, but I will do my best.

PREPARATION TIME
00 : 00 : 45

RESPONSE TIME
00 : 00 : 45

GO ON TO THE NEXT PAGE.

Question 2: Read a Text Aloud

 **Question 2**

Directions: In this part of the test, you will read aloud the text on the screen. You will have 45 seconds to prepare. Then you will have 45 seconds to read the text aloud.

The life of a career academic or postgraduate student typically does not lend itself easily to vacation and travel, making the opportunity to attend a scientific conference an attractive benefit. A conference is a great opportunity to meet people in your field and put faces to names from publications. It is a great opportunity to network and meet the leaders in your field, collaborators, and potential supervisors or graduate students. Conferences also enable researchers to keep abreast of all advances in their field by presenting the latest research on a variety of subjects.

PREPARATION TIME
00 : 00 : 45

RESPONSE TIME
00 : 00 : 45

Question 3: Describe a Picture

 **Question 3**

Directions: In this part of the test, you will describe the picture on your screen in as much detail as you can. You will have 30 seconds to prepare your response. Then you will have 45 seconds to speak about the picture.

PREPARATION TIME
00 : 00 : 30

RESPONSE TIME
00 : 00 : 45

GO ON TO THE NEXT PAGE.

Question 3: Describe a Picture

答題範例

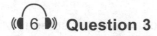 **Question 3**

Three young children are posing for a picture.

They appear to be healthy.

They appear to be happy.

Two of the children are wearing headscarves.

One of the children is covering his or her face.

He or she might be camera-shy.

The child on the left looks a lot like the child in the middle.

Maybe they are siblings.

They almost look like twins.

The background is a dry and barren landscape.

It's probably in the desert.

There is nothing to indicate where they might be.

The children have brown skin.

They also have dark eyes.

All three are wearing jewelry such as bracelets and necklaces.

At least one child has multiple ear-piercings.

I'd say this is in the Middle East or Central Asia.

Another possibility is South America.

Questions 4-6: Respond to Questions

 **Question 4**

Directions: In this part of the test, you will answer three questions. For each question, begin responding immediately after you hear a beep. No preparation time is provided. You will have 15 seconds to respond to Questions 4 and 5 and 30 seconds to respond to Question 6.

Imagine that a British marketing firm is doing research in your country. You have agreed to answer some questions in a telephone interview about your diet.

Question 4
On a scale of 1 to 10, how healthy is your diet?

RESPONSE TIME
00 : 00 : 15

Question 5
How much attention do you pay to nutritional information on packaged foods?

RESPONSE TIME
00 : 00 : 15

Question 6
Describe your favorite meal or type of food.

RESPONSE TIME
00 : 00 : 30

GO ON TO THE NEXT PAGE.

Questions 4-6: Respond to Questions

答題範例

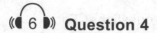 **Question 4**

On a scale of 1 to 10, how healthy is your diet?

Answer

> I'd say I'm about a 5.
>
> I try to eat as healthy as possible.
>
> But I'm sure there's room for improvement.

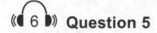 **Question 5**

How much attention do you pay to nutritional information on packaged foods?

Answer

> Not that much, honestly.
>
> Occasionally, I'll read the label.
>
> I sometimes check for sodium content.

Questions 4-6: Respond to Questions

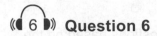 **Question 6**

Describe your favorite meal or type of food.

Answer

> My favorite type of cuisine is Chinese.
>
> No other type of food comes close.
>
> It is my comfort food.
>
>
> Chinese cuisine is very versatile.
>
> There are very light dishes like a simple noodle soup.
>
> There are also very hearty dishes, for instance, hot pot.
>
>
> Chinese cuisine emphasizes freshness and flavor.
>
> Only the best ingredients are used.
>
> Every dish is prepared with great care.

GO ON TO THE NEXT PAGE.

Questions 7-9: Respond to Questions Using Information Provided

 **Question 7**

Directions: In this part of the test, you will answer three questions based on the information provided. You will have 30 seconds to read the information before the questions begin. For each question, begin responding immediately after you hear a beep. No additional preparation time is provided. You will have 15 seconds to respond to Questions 7 and 8 and 30 seconds to respond to Question 9.

FREE SEMINAR*
Pet Grooming Training

Do you have a cat or a dog with a shaggy coat of fur? Are you tired of paying expensive grooming fees? Would you like to learn how to groom your pet yourself? Learn how to turn the anxiety of grooming into a bonding time for you and your pet. We will teach you:

NAIL AND FUR MAINTENENCE • DENTAL CARE • MASSAGE THERAPY

Who are we?

Danny and Tanya Smith are an animal loving couple who have volunteered their time for the protection of animals for more than 20 years. Their San Francisco-based pet spa Pampered Paws was voted #1 in the animal care category for Northern California's Best Small Businesses four years in a row (2008-2011).

How to attend?

Visit our website: www.pawspetspa.com for more information
or call Danny Smith at (415)454-2222

*Reservations required. Though this event is offered free of charge, the organizers ask that you bring a pet food (or monetary) donation for the local animal shelter.

Hi, I'm interested in the free pet grooming seminar. May I ask a few questions?

PREPARATION TIME

00 : 00 : 30

Question 7

RESPONSE TIME

00 : 00 : 15

Question 8

RESPONSE TIME

00 : 00 : 15

Question 9

RESPONSE TIME

00 : 00 : 30

Questions 7-9: Respond to Questions Using Information Provided

答題範例

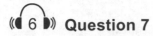 **Question 7**

What kind of experience do you have with animals?

Answer

> My wife and I have been involved with animals for over 20 years.
>
> We own and operate the Pampered Pets animal spa.
>
> Pampered Pets has been voted Northern California's #1 Small Business four years in a row.

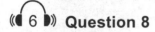 **Question 8**

My dog's fur is always matted and tangled. Will there be any tips to deal with this problem?

Answer

> Yes.
>
> We will be showing you how to shampoo and bathe your pet properly.
>
> We will also show you how to prevent your dog's fur from matting.

GO ON TO THE NEXT PAGE.

Questions 7-9: Respond to Questions Using Information Provided

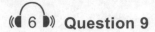 **Question 9**

Is there a fee for the seminar?

Answer

The seminar itself is free.

Tanya and I do this in our free time.

It's not about making money.

However, we do require registration.

That's just so we know you'll be there.

We don't want to waste anybody's time.

Meanwhile, we do ask that participants bring a donation

for the animal shelter.

This could be pet food or money.

There are some other ideas for donations on our Web

site.

Question 10: Propose a Solution

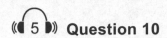 **Question 10**

Directions: In this part of the test, you will be presented with a problem and asked to propose a solution. You will have 30 seconds to prepare. Then you will have 60 seconds to speak. In your response, be sure to show that you recognize the problem, and propose a way of dealing with the problem.

In your response, be sure to
- show that you recognize the caller's problem, and
- propose a way of dealing with the problem.

PREPARATION TIME
00 : 00 : 30

RESPONSE TIME
00 : 01 : 00

GO ON TO THE NEXT PAGE.

Question 10: Propose a Solution

答題範例

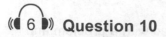 **Question 10**

Voice Message

Hi, this is Steve calling for Todd. It's about three on Friday afternoon. Listen, Todd. I had something come up at the last-minute, so I won't be able to meet with you and Sandra on Monday as we had planned. I'd like to reschedule for later in the week, if that works for you and Sandra. I'm available late Tuesday and Thursday afternoons, but early morning Wednesday or Friday would actually be best for me. We could still meet at Sandra's office, as we planned, or I'd be able to meet somewhere else if it's more convenient for you. Sorry about the cancellation. Please call me as soon as you can after hearing this. My cell is 886-2468, or you can call my office at 351-9823 and leave a message. Thanks, Todd. I'll talk to you soon.

Question 10: Propose a Solution

答題範例

Hello Steve.

I got your message and I'm returning your call.

Rescheduling is not a problem.

As it turns out, I would have had to cancel the meeting anyway.

Something came up on my end, too.

So don't apologize.

Let me check with Sandra about next week.

I know her schedule is pretty full.

But I'm sure we can work something out.

Ideally, we could meet Thursday afternoon.

Later in the week works best for me.

It gives me a little more breathing room.

We'll meet in Sandra's office as originally planned.

I think that's best for everyone.

And she has video conferencing in case we want to contact the investors.

So let's play it by ear.

Give me a call on Monday, by which time I'll have talked to Sandra.

Enjoy your weekend.

GO ON TO THE NEXT PAGE.

Question 11: Express an Opinion

Directions: In this part of the test, you will give your opinion about a specific topic. Be sure to say as much as you can in the time allowed. You will have 15 seconds to prepare. Then you will have 60 seconds to speak.

Some people prefer to live in warm climates all year round. However, studies show that crime rates are much higher in warmer climates. Do you think that people in warm climates lead happier lives or not? State your opinion and provide reasons for support.

PREPARATION TIME
00 : 00 : 15

RESPONSE TIME
00 : 01 : 00

Question 11: Express an Opinion

答題範例

 **Question 11**

I think a certain balance is the key to a happy life.

This applies to everything, including the weather.

Sometimes you can have too much of a good thing.

When it is sunny for too long, people head to the shade.

But, if it rains for a few days, people complain.

It's a lose-lose situation.

I think extremely cold weather can make people miserable, though.

When it is too cold, you shiver.

You can't go outside and all your energy is spent trying to get warm.

However, you have to take the good with the bad.

Higher crimes rates are a trade-off for comfortable weather.

I would think that people in warmer climates understand this.

Personally, I think people in warmer climates may be happier.

They have one less thing to worry about: staying comfortable.

It's just my opinion but it's easier to smile when the sun's shining.

People in cold climates tend to be conservative.

They also tend to have narrow minds.

They don't seem happy to me.

GO ON TO THE NEXT PAGE.

NO TEST MATERIAL ON THIS PAGE

New TOEIC Writing Test

Questions 1-5: Write a Sentence Based on a Picture

Question 1

Directions: Write ONE sentence based on the picture using the TWO words or phrases under it. You may change the forms of the words and you may use them in any order.

dog / surfboard

GO ON TO THE NEXT PAGE.

Questions 1-5: Write a Sentence Based on a Picture

Question 2

Directions: Write ONE sentence based on the picture using the TWO words or phrases under it. You may change the forms of the words and you may use them in any order.

board / children

Questions 1-5: Write a Sentence Based on a Picture

Question 3

Directions: Write ONE sentence based on the picture using the TWO words or phrases under it. You may change the forms of the words and you may use them in any order.

music / students

GO ON TO THE NEXT PAGE.

Questions 1-5: Write a Sentence Based on a Picture

Question 4

Directions: Write ONE sentence based on the picture using the TWO words or phrases under it. You may change the forms of the words and you may use them in any order.

couple / married

Questions 1-5: Write a Sentence Based on a Picture

Question 5

Directions: Write ONE sentence based on the picture using the TWO words or phrases under it. You may change the forms of the words and you may use them in any order.

airport / gates

GO ON TO THE NEXT PAGE.

Questions 6-7: Respond to a written request

Question 6

Directions: Read the e-mail below.

From: Kane Lightfoot <k_lightfoot@coheed.com>
To: Rani Ahmad <r_ahmad@inmail.com>
Re: Part-time opportunity
Sent: January 31

Dear Ms. Ahmad,

We sincerely appreciate you interviewing for the senior Web administrator position at Coheed & Associates. However, I regret to inform you that the personnel department decided to go with another candidate. Nevertheless, we were impressed by the knowledge and experience that you displayed during your interview and have decided to offer you another recently-vacated position.

In contrast to the position you applied for, this position is part-time. You would be working on Tuesday, Wednesday, and Friday from 1:00 to 5:00 PM and on Monday and Thursday from 2:00 to 6:00 PM.

If you are interested in this position, please call me at 555-0923 or email me at k_lightfoot@coheed.com.

Sincerely,
Kane Lightfoot

Directions: Write back to Mr. Lightfoot and accept the position, but request ONE minor change to the scheduled work hours. Give ONE reason for the request.

Questions 6-7: Respond to a written request

答題範例

Question 6

Dear Mr. Lightfoot,

Thank you for your letter of January 31. It's unfortunate that the position I applied for has been filled, but I would be very pleased to accept the new position that you are offering. However, I was wondering if you would be agreeable to a minor change regarding the hours I would be working.

During my interview, I referenced my experience volunteering with World Vision. I was recently offered a position working part time for them, but there is a schedule conflict. I work for them Tuesday, Wednesday, and Thursday from 9:00 AM to 1:00 PM. Would it be possible for me to work for you from 1:30 to 5:30 PM on Tuesday and Wednesday? If so, please let me know at your earliest convenience.

Incidentally, the duties that I currently perform for World Vision are exactly the same as the responsibilities of the position with Coheed & Associates. So, I believe that I would adjust very quickly to working for Coheed.

I look forward to becoming a valuable member of Coheed & Associates.

Sincerely,
Rani Ahmad

GO ON TO THE NEXT PAGE.

Question 7

Directions: Read the e-mail below.

From: Shirley Jackson <cc_jackson@shaker.com>
To: Sunburst Airlines Claims <claims@sunburstairline.com>
Date: June 15
Subject: Claim # SA345
Attachments: jackson.jpg; jackson2.jpg; jackson3.jpg

To whom it may concern:

On May 19, I traveled from Newark, New Jersey, to Orlando, Florida, on Sunburst Airlines Flight 810. My bag arrived on a different flight and was delivered to my home only a few hours ago. The contents were fine, but the exterior of the bag was badly damaged. The case was dented. The suitcase is no longer usable as it cannot be closed properly. On May 21, I submitted claim form number SA345. I understood that I would take up to two weeks for the claim to be processed, but it is now June 15 and I have not had any response.

Please let me know how this problem will be resolved. As I did with the original claim, I am attaching a photo of the damaged property and photocopies of my boarding pass and baggage claim tickets.

Shirley Jackson

Directions: Reply to Ms. Jackson as Kirby Little, Claims Manager of Sunburst Airlines. Tell her that you've resolved her issue and offer ONE thing in return for the inconvenience. Also include TWO ways of contacting you.

Questions 6-7: Respond to a written request

答題範例

Question 7

Ms. Jackson,

Thank you for submitting your claim to Sunburst Airlines. We deeply regret the delay in processing your request. After reviewing the documentation, I have approved your claim and have issued full restitution for both losing and damaging your baggage. A check for the total amount has been mailed to the address listed on your original flight reservation. In light of the inconvenience, I have taken the liberty of including an Sunburst Airlines Voucher of $200 value toward a flight ticket redeemable within the next six months.

Thank you for being a Sunburst Airlines passenger. If you have any questions or concerns, please contact me directly either by email or the number below.

Kirby Little
Claims Manager
(800)774-3300 ext. 98

GO ON TO THE NEXT PAGE.

Questions 8: Write an opinion essay

Question 8

Directions: Read the question below. You have 30 minutes to plan, write, and revise your essay. Typically, an effective response will contain a minimum of 300 words.

Think about a job you have had or would like to have. In your opinion, what are the most important characteristics that you and the people you work with should possess to be successful in that job? Use reasons and specific examples to illustrate why these characteristics are important.

Questions 8: Write an opinion essay

答題範例

Question 8

There is no recipe for success in farming, but experts agree certain qualities set successful farmers and ranchers apart, including passion, a positive attitude, the ability to handle adversity and "gut instinct." Successful producers also embrace change and maintain a can-do attitude. When problems arise, they come up with solutions instead of excuses. They also have a good understanding of local and global markets and the issues facing their industry.

The first quality of a successful farmer is learning how to manage money. Most farmers start small, keeping costs down and doing a lot of the construction work themselves. People in business need to start small with any new venture so that the mistakes are small enough that they can adjust and survive.

Next, innovation has always been a big part of farming. The ups and downs of growing commodity crops have become more frequent and severe. Taking a different path and producing for markets with specific needs offers a better chance at evening out the peaks and valleys. The ability to adapt to market changes is key; resourcefulness will help a business survive when times are tough.

Third, time management is important in any business, but it's crucial in farming, where outside factors such as weather have a huge impact. Whether it's bad weather or equipment breakdowns, a producer has to be ready to switch from plan A to plan B, or C or D.

Fourth, as a business gets larger, strong communication and people skills are also necessary so every part of the operation is being managed properly. Good operators have other good people in their corner. Playing to your strengths improves efficiencies and saves headaches. Hire someone who's good at the things you're not good at or don't care to do.

Finally, the most important quality of a farmer is attention to detail. A dairy farmer, for example, must always be checking cows, milk charts, rations, feed costs and markets——keeping abreast of everything and looking for areas that can be improved. You have to pay attention to the growing side of things for peak production, but marketing a product also demands a great deal of time and attention to detail. Producing, processing, and marketing produce requires both physical and mental attention. It's attention to small details that makes you or breaks you. If you don't pay attention to the small details, they can turn into large problems. Given the high price of agricultural products, mistakes are very expensive.

TOEIC 練習測驗 答案紙

LISTENING SECTION

Part 1

No.	ANSWER (A B C D)
1	Ⓐ Ⓑ Ⓒ Ⓓ
2	Ⓐ Ⓑ Ⓒ Ⓓ
3	Ⓐ Ⓑ Ⓒ Ⓓ
4	Ⓐ Ⓑ Ⓒ Ⓓ
5	Ⓐ Ⓑ Ⓒ Ⓓ
6	Ⓐ Ⓑ Ⓒ Ⓓ
7	Ⓐ Ⓑ Ⓒ Ⓓ
8	Ⓐ Ⓑ Ⓒ Ⓓ
9	Ⓐ Ⓑ Ⓒ Ⓓ
10	Ⓐ Ⓑ Ⓒ Ⓓ

Part 2

No.	ANSWER (A B C)
11	Ⓐ Ⓑ Ⓒ
12	Ⓐ Ⓑ Ⓒ
13	Ⓐ Ⓑ Ⓒ
14	Ⓐ Ⓑ Ⓒ
15	Ⓐ Ⓑ Ⓒ
16	Ⓐ Ⓑ Ⓒ
17	Ⓐ Ⓑ Ⓒ
18	Ⓐ Ⓑ Ⓒ
19	Ⓐ Ⓑ Ⓒ
20	Ⓐ Ⓑ Ⓒ
21	Ⓐ Ⓑ Ⓒ
22	Ⓐ Ⓑ Ⓒ
23	Ⓐ Ⓑ Ⓒ
24	Ⓐ Ⓑ Ⓒ
25	Ⓐ Ⓑ Ⓒ
26	Ⓐ Ⓑ Ⓒ
27	Ⓐ Ⓑ Ⓒ
28	Ⓐ Ⓑ Ⓒ
29	Ⓐ Ⓑ Ⓒ
30	Ⓐ Ⓑ Ⓒ

Part 3

No.	ANSWER (A B C D)
31	Ⓐ Ⓑ Ⓒ Ⓓ
32	Ⓐ Ⓑ Ⓒ Ⓓ
33	Ⓐ Ⓑ Ⓒ Ⓓ
34	Ⓐ Ⓑ Ⓒ Ⓓ
35	Ⓐ Ⓑ Ⓒ Ⓓ
36	Ⓐ Ⓑ Ⓒ Ⓓ
37	Ⓐ Ⓑ Ⓒ Ⓓ
38	Ⓐ Ⓑ Ⓒ Ⓓ
39	Ⓐ Ⓑ Ⓒ Ⓓ
40	Ⓐ Ⓑ Ⓒ Ⓓ
41	Ⓐ Ⓑ Ⓒ Ⓓ
42	Ⓐ Ⓑ Ⓒ Ⓓ
43	Ⓐ Ⓑ Ⓒ Ⓓ
44	Ⓐ Ⓑ Ⓒ Ⓓ
45	Ⓐ Ⓑ Ⓒ Ⓓ
46	Ⓐ Ⓑ Ⓒ Ⓓ
47	Ⓐ Ⓑ Ⓒ Ⓓ
48	Ⓐ Ⓑ Ⓒ Ⓓ
49	Ⓐ Ⓑ Ⓒ Ⓓ
50	Ⓐ Ⓑ Ⓒ Ⓓ
51	Ⓐ Ⓑ Ⓒ Ⓓ
52	Ⓐ Ⓑ Ⓒ Ⓓ
53	Ⓐ Ⓑ Ⓒ Ⓓ
54	Ⓐ Ⓑ Ⓒ Ⓓ
55	Ⓐ Ⓑ Ⓒ Ⓓ
56	Ⓐ Ⓑ Ⓒ Ⓓ
57	Ⓐ Ⓑ Ⓒ Ⓓ
58	Ⓐ Ⓑ Ⓒ Ⓓ
59	Ⓐ Ⓑ Ⓒ Ⓓ
60	Ⓐ Ⓑ Ⓒ Ⓓ
61	Ⓐ Ⓑ Ⓒ Ⓓ
62	Ⓐ Ⓑ Ⓒ Ⓓ
63	Ⓐ Ⓑ Ⓒ Ⓓ
64	Ⓐ Ⓑ Ⓒ Ⓓ
65	Ⓐ Ⓑ Ⓒ Ⓓ
66	Ⓐ Ⓑ Ⓒ Ⓓ
67	Ⓐ Ⓑ Ⓒ Ⓓ
68	Ⓐ Ⓑ Ⓒ Ⓓ
69	Ⓐ Ⓑ Ⓒ Ⓓ
70	Ⓐ Ⓑ Ⓒ Ⓓ

Part 4

No.	ANSWER (A B C D)
71	Ⓐ Ⓑ Ⓒ Ⓓ
72	Ⓐ Ⓑ Ⓒ Ⓓ
73	Ⓐ Ⓑ Ⓒ Ⓓ
74	Ⓐ Ⓑ Ⓒ Ⓓ
75	Ⓐ Ⓑ Ⓒ Ⓓ
76	Ⓐ Ⓑ Ⓒ Ⓓ
77	Ⓐ Ⓑ Ⓒ Ⓓ
78	Ⓐ Ⓑ Ⓒ Ⓓ
79	Ⓐ Ⓑ Ⓒ Ⓓ
80	Ⓐ Ⓑ Ⓒ Ⓓ
81	Ⓐ Ⓑ Ⓒ Ⓓ
82	Ⓐ Ⓑ Ⓒ Ⓓ
83	Ⓐ Ⓑ Ⓒ Ⓓ
84	Ⓐ Ⓑ Ⓒ Ⓓ
85	Ⓐ Ⓑ Ⓒ Ⓓ
86	Ⓐ Ⓑ Ⓒ Ⓓ
87	Ⓐ Ⓑ Ⓒ Ⓓ
88	Ⓐ Ⓑ Ⓒ Ⓓ
89	Ⓐ Ⓑ Ⓒ Ⓓ
90	Ⓐ Ⓑ Ⓒ Ⓓ
91	Ⓐ Ⓑ Ⓒ Ⓓ
92	Ⓐ Ⓑ Ⓒ Ⓓ
93	Ⓐ Ⓑ Ⓒ Ⓓ
94	Ⓐ Ⓑ Ⓒ Ⓓ
95	Ⓐ Ⓑ Ⓒ Ⓓ
96	Ⓐ Ⓑ Ⓒ Ⓓ
97	Ⓐ Ⓑ Ⓒ Ⓓ
98	Ⓐ Ⓑ Ⓒ Ⓓ
99	Ⓐ Ⓑ Ⓒ Ⓓ
100	Ⓐ Ⓑ Ⓒ Ⓓ

READING SECTION

Part 5

No.	ANSWER (A B C D)
101	Ⓐ Ⓑ Ⓒ Ⓓ
102	Ⓐ Ⓑ Ⓒ Ⓓ
103	Ⓐ Ⓑ Ⓒ Ⓓ
104	Ⓐ Ⓑ Ⓒ Ⓓ
105	Ⓐ Ⓑ Ⓒ Ⓓ
106	Ⓐ Ⓑ Ⓒ Ⓓ
107	Ⓐ Ⓑ Ⓒ Ⓓ
108	Ⓐ Ⓑ Ⓒ Ⓓ
109	Ⓐ Ⓑ Ⓒ Ⓓ
110	Ⓐ Ⓑ Ⓒ Ⓓ
111	Ⓐ Ⓑ Ⓒ Ⓓ
112	Ⓐ Ⓑ Ⓒ Ⓓ
113	Ⓐ Ⓑ Ⓒ Ⓓ
114	Ⓐ Ⓑ Ⓒ Ⓓ
115	Ⓐ Ⓑ Ⓒ Ⓓ
116	Ⓐ Ⓑ Ⓒ Ⓓ
117	Ⓐ Ⓑ Ⓒ Ⓓ
118	Ⓐ Ⓑ Ⓒ Ⓓ
119	Ⓐ Ⓑ Ⓒ Ⓓ
120	Ⓐ Ⓑ Ⓒ Ⓓ
121	Ⓐ Ⓑ Ⓒ Ⓓ
122	Ⓐ Ⓑ Ⓒ Ⓓ
123	Ⓐ Ⓑ Ⓒ Ⓓ
124	Ⓐ Ⓑ Ⓒ Ⓓ
125	Ⓐ Ⓑ Ⓒ Ⓓ
126	Ⓐ Ⓑ Ⓒ Ⓓ
127	Ⓐ Ⓑ Ⓒ Ⓓ
128	Ⓐ Ⓑ Ⓒ Ⓓ
129	Ⓐ Ⓑ Ⓒ Ⓓ
130	Ⓐ Ⓑ Ⓒ Ⓓ

Part 6

No.	ANSWER (A B C D)
131	Ⓐ Ⓑ Ⓒ Ⓓ
132	Ⓐ Ⓑ Ⓒ Ⓓ
133	Ⓐ Ⓑ Ⓒ Ⓓ
134	Ⓐ Ⓑ Ⓒ Ⓓ
135	Ⓐ Ⓑ Ⓒ Ⓓ
136	Ⓐ Ⓑ Ⓒ Ⓓ
137	Ⓐ Ⓑ Ⓒ Ⓓ
138	Ⓐ Ⓑ Ⓒ Ⓓ
139	Ⓐ Ⓑ Ⓒ Ⓓ
140	Ⓐ Ⓑ Ⓒ Ⓓ

Part 7

No.	ANSWER (A B C D)
141	Ⓐ Ⓑ Ⓒ Ⓓ
142	Ⓐ Ⓑ Ⓒ Ⓓ
143	Ⓐ Ⓑ Ⓒ Ⓓ
144	Ⓐ Ⓑ Ⓒ Ⓓ
145	Ⓐ Ⓑ Ⓒ Ⓓ
146	Ⓐ Ⓑ Ⓒ Ⓓ
147	Ⓐ Ⓑ Ⓒ Ⓓ
148	Ⓐ Ⓑ Ⓒ Ⓓ
149	Ⓐ Ⓑ Ⓒ Ⓓ
150	Ⓐ Ⓑ Ⓒ Ⓓ
151	Ⓐ Ⓑ Ⓒ Ⓓ
152	Ⓐ Ⓑ Ⓒ Ⓓ
153	Ⓐ Ⓑ Ⓒ Ⓓ
154	Ⓐ Ⓑ Ⓒ Ⓓ
155	Ⓐ Ⓑ Ⓒ Ⓓ
156	Ⓐ Ⓑ Ⓒ Ⓓ
157	Ⓐ Ⓑ Ⓒ Ⓓ
158	Ⓐ Ⓑ Ⓒ Ⓓ
159	Ⓐ Ⓑ Ⓒ Ⓓ
160	Ⓐ Ⓑ Ⓒ Ⓓ
161	Ⓐ Ⓑ Ⓒ Ⓓ
162	Ⓐ Ⓑ Ⓒ Ⓓ
163	Ⓐ Ⓑ Ⓒ Ⓓ
164	Ⓐ Ⓑ Ⓒ Ⓓ
165	Ⓐ Ⓑ Ⓒ Ⓓ
166	Ⓐ Ⓑ Ⓒ Ⓓ
167	Ⓐ Ⓑ Ⓒ Ⓓ
168	Ⓐ Ⓑ Ⓒ Ⓓ
169	Ⓐ Ⓑ Ⓒ Ⓓ
170	Ⓐ Ⓑ Ⓒ Ⓓ
171	Ⓐ Ⓑ Ⓒ Ⓓ
172	Ⓐ Ⓑ Ⓒ Ⓓ
173	Ⓐ Ⓑ Ⓒ Ⓓ
174	Ⓐ Ⓑ Ⓒ Ⓓ
175	Ⓐ Ⓑ Ⓒ Ⓓ
176	Ⓐ Ⓑ Ⓒ Ⓓ
177	Ⓐ Ⓑ Ⓒ Ⓓ
178	Ⓐ Ⓑ Ⓒ Ⓓ
179	Ⓐ Ⓑ Ⓒ Ⓓ
180	Ⓐ Ⓑ Ⓒ Ⓓ
181	Ⓐ Ⓑ Ⓒ Ⓓ
182	Ⓐ Ⓑ Ⓒ Ⓓ
183	Ⓐ Ⓑ Ⓒ Ⓓ
184	Ⓐ Ⓑ Ⓒ Ⓓ
185	Ⓐ Ⓑ Ⓒ Ⓓ
186	Ⓐ Ⓑ Ⓒ Ⓓ
187	Ⓐ Ⓑ Ⓒ Ⓓ
188	Ⓐ Ⓑ Ⓒ Ⓓ
189	Ⓐ Ⓑ Ⓒ Ⓓ
190	Ⓐ Ⓑ Ⓒ Ⓓ
191	Ⓐ Ⓑ Ⓒ Ⓓ
192	Ⓐ Ⓑ Ⓒ Ⓓ
193	Ⓐ Ⓑ Ⓒ Ⓓ
194	Ⓐ Ⓑ Ⓒ Ⓓ
195	Ⓐ Ⓑ Ⓒ Ⓓ
196	Ⓐ Ⓑ Ⓒ Ⓓ
197	Ⓐ Ⓑ Ⓒ Ⓓ
198	Ⓐ Ⓑ Ⓒ Ⓓ
199	Ⓐ Ⓑ Ⓒ Ⓓ
200	Ⓐ Ⓑ Ⓒ Ⓓ